CHRIS ALMEIDA &
CECILIA AUBREY

COUNTERMEASURE:
BYTES OF LIFE

VOLUME I

Contents

Praise for CHRIS ALMEIDA AND CECILIA AUBREY:

"A riveting, clever spy story full of intrigue, modern-day espionage and a scorching hot romance."

—*Misty Evans, award-winning author of romantic suspense*

"If you like nonstop action and sexy heroes and heroines, don't miss the Countermeasure Series."

—*Desiree Holt, best-selling author or erotic romance*

"Almeida and Aubrey had me from the first paragraph and I couldn't put it down. Electrifying thriller!"

—*Becky Condit, Mrs Condit and Friends Read Books*

"It is beautifully written with the perfect mixture of action and suspense and in the midst of all that there is a beautiful emotional love story entwined."

—*Rhayne Risque, Guilty Pleasures Book Reviews*

"I highly recommend Countermeasure for any fan of a fast paced erotic romance. I know I'm looking forward to checking out the duo's next collaboration!"

—*Silla Beaumont, Just Erotic Romance Reviews*

ISBN 978-1-927554-22-7
ALL RIGHTS RESERVED
Ecstasy by the Sea © 2012 Chris Almeida & Cecilia Aubrey/ Éire Publishing, LLC
Cuffed at Midnight © 2012 Chris Almeida & Cecilia Aubrey/ Éire Publishing, LLC
Passion at Dawn © 2012 Chris Almeida & Cecilia Aubrey/ Éire Publishing, LLC
Edited by Emmanuelle Hertel
Cover art by Chris Almeida
Electronic book publication October 2012

TRADEMARK ACKNOWLEDGEMENTS

The authors acknowledge the trademarked status and trademark owners of the following wordmarks mentioned in this work of fiction:

Star Wars, Yoda, Imperial March: LucasArts

Highlander, the movie: Summit Entertainment

Waterside House Hotel Dublin: Waterside House Hotel Dublin

Guinness: Diageo Ireland Private Unlimited Company

Cosmopolitan Magazine: Hearst Communications, Inc.

Sligo Rovers: Sligo Rovers F. C.

ECSTASY BY THE SEA

"He's more myself than I am. Whatever our souls are made of, his and mine are the same."

—Emily Brontë

Chapter One

Reminiscences

T HE FLIGHT FROM CALIFORNIA TO Ireland via New York was long. Trevor leaned his head against the headrest and couldn't strip the smile from his face during the whole journey even if he wanted to. Married. To Cassandra. What would the future have in store for them? So much had happened to bring them together. So much pain, fear—but also joy and love. Once he had broken through Cassandra's walls, she had given herself to him fully, completely.

He turned his head and let his eyes roam over her sleeping figure, travel along the soft golden sun-kissed skin, the curve of her neck, her full lips. His body awakened again and temptation reared its insatiable head. He leaned over and kissed her lips softly. She didn't move.

The day had been tiring and she was out for the count. So serene. He studied the shape of her eyes, so much like her father's. Robert James, or

Bob, as Cassandra called him, was a force to be reckoned with. Over the last couple of months, the ex-Navy Seal and some of his buddies had put Trevor through the ringer. After the initial dress-down Trevor had given Robert in France, they had toed the line. Robert consistently tested him, drilled him, almost as if to assure himself that Trevor was worthy of Cassandra.

His cronies were even worse—like overprotective uncles. Trevor had finally won their approval over a game of paintball. He might be a geek, but he was one hell of a single-shooter video game player—and wasn't paintball just a game like those he and George played just about every day? Poor George had fallen within the first few minutes. Matt, the Boy Wonder, another die-hard gamer, on the other hand, had become his brother-in-arms, and together they had held their own until the end of the motley crew's warped version of a bachelor party. He'd won the respect of the men by shooting them all dead—figuratively speaking, of course. Go figure. Cassandra still shook her head over that episode and the bruises he had sported as badges of honor just days before the wedding.

A victorious smile tipped the corners of his mouth and he eased back in his seat, absorbed by a series of thoughts and reminiscences. And gratitude to Stephan.

Two nights before the wedding, he and Stephan had been sitting on the patio of the Irish Bank, a traditional Irish pub in the heart of downtown San Francisco. Cassandra had introduced him to the bar on his first night in town. With its homey interior and comfortable mix of barstools and wooden tables, the pub had been the perfect place for him and Stephan to unwind and chat after not having talked face to face in a long while.

They had been enjoying a pint when Stephan had dropped a bomb of a question. *"Where are you taking Cassandra for your honeymoon?"*

"Honeymoon?" Trevor's eyes had grown wide as he'd stared dumbfounded at Stephan. Overtaken by the flurry of activity around getting all the loose ends tied before setting foot in Ireland, he and Cassandra had completely missed the boat on that one. How could he have totally ignored one of the most important adventures in a new marriage? Even more

surprising was that Cassandra had not mentioned a word during all the planning—and anybody who knew Cassandra knew what a stickler for detail she was.

The wedding, the move, the renovations on the house, his new position with the NSA had taken up all the space in his mind. Disappointment had torn at his insides. That had been a hell of a fail. Understanding had flooded Stephan's eyes.

"You didn't plan anything? You'd better scramble."

Trevor had looked at him helplessly, running his fingers repeatedly through his hair. *"Shite! This is a mess. What can be done on such short notice?"*

Stephan had clapped him on the back in sympathy and pulled out his cell. *"I'll have Máire email you some suggestions on where you can take Cassandra. It's late, but she will be thrilled to help. I am sure with some persuasion you can get this planned before you tie the knot."*

Máire, Trevor's father's efficient secretary, had assisted Stephan since Conor Brennan's disappearance. Luckily, she had pulled through and had handled the details once he had picked an option out of the few she had provided. As hard as it had been to have kept that secret from Cassandra, he knew they would both enjoy the results of his little surprise.

Too keyed-up to sleep, he settled for an in-flight movie, but an hour later he was still unable to focus on the rerun of one of Hollywood's latest blockbuster. His buzzing thoughts centered on their wedding, a new beginning, a new life with Cassandra. New responsibilities.

He had contemplated all of that before, dwelling on the repercussions of giving his heart so entirely. The burden of his quest, his search for the truth, was not a light one; it was what had kept him from her when they first met. But she had accepted it all. Accepted him, his baggage, his need to find closure—even his freaking dreams and nightmares. He wanted to make it all good, find the answers he needed so the two of them could move on. He wanted them to be a normal couple, the kind that would have barbecues and get-togethers with friends regularly, vacations abroad for pleasure—not a nosedive into another deadly adventure like the last one. They would become that normal couple—once he had, they had, answers. That was the only certainty in his mind.

He regretted that his parents had never met Cassandra. A longing pang struck deep and he squeezed his eyes shut. Trevor missed the two of them dearly. They would have loved her on the spot, and she would have loved them in return. He knew his mother would have taken Cassandra under her wing, given her the mother's love Cassandra missed and needed. A soft chuckle escaped him at hearing his parents badgering him in his head, urging them to start their own family as soon as they set foot in Ireland, his mother begging for a grandchild to spoil.

Trevor's eyes grew damp imagining them as grandparents, and his lips quirked in a half-grin thinking of how spoiled their child would have been. His heart ached with sadness, knowing that those wonderful thoughts would forever live solely in his mind.

He turned to face his dozing wife and gently eased a stray strand of silky auburn hair behind the delicate shell of her ear. Wherever the next step of their journey led them, he was glad they were facing it together. Somehow, that knowledge made the prospect of whatever he uncovered regarding his parents' disappearance a bit more bearable. The first step in their new adventure, Ireland: the country of his birth and their new home. Trevor leaned his head against the seat and tried to shut down and recharge for what lay ahead.

Chapter Two

Home Sweet Home

TWO CONNECTIONS AND SOME THIRTEEN hours later, they arrived in beautiful Ireland. Stephan had been a great help in the past months, overseeing the renovations in their Georgian home across from St. Stephen's Green, and had even arranged for their pickup at the airport.

Trevor dropped their luggage on the step and unlocked the massive door.

As he pushed it open, Cassandra reached for one of the bags. Before she had time to react, Trevor swept her off her feet. "What are—?"

He grinned and took a giant step, carrying her over the threshold. Her laughter bubbled over at his old-fashioned gesture. Once he set her back on her feet in the foyer, she cradled his face with her hands and kissed him. "I love you."

He grinned wickedly back. "I know." Returning the quick peck on the lips, he rushed outside for their luggage and followed Cassandra as she climbed the stairs to the first level.

She stopped by the archway to the first floor and took in the fabulous space. "Wow. It's even more beautiful than the pictures and videos Stephan sent us." Warm golden wood flooring covered the open-concept area. The kitchen was the perfect size, with dark chocolate-tone wood cabinets, brushed silver hardware, and cream granite countertops threaded with dark veins that complemented the chocolaty cabinets. Cassandra walked into the kitchen and brushed her hand over the cool surface of the counters and the white subway tiling on the wall. "Nice! Stephan actually pulled off exactly what we asked for."

"Yep. The seventy-inch flat screen I have been drooling over looks awesome mounted on the wall."

"Great movie nights ahead, for sure." He watched Cassandra's eyes pass over the big screen embedded in a large media center surrounded by speakers and every electronic gadget Trevor had lusted after. She grinned and nodded toward the couch. "Even the couch has a nice deep seat for snuggling."

Trevor waggled his eyebrows. "Oh, yeah! And did you see the front door? The restoration results were brilliant. All of the original Georgian details are now showing."

Cassandra chuckled at his enthusiasm. "One would think you were talking about the Mona Lisa."

"Hey! That's an authentic Georgian door! And, considering where we live, it had to be one."

Most of the houses around St. Stephen's Green still retained the classical façades from the Georgian era and sported the traditional bright colored doors that marked the period.

She shook her head. "Love when you get all geeky about things."

He closed the distance and circled her waist with an arm, pulling her closer. "Should I begin to talk geek now? I know how it turns you on: uploads…." He cupped her face and kissed her lips in a slow, deliberate touch, nipping at her full lower lip.

"Mmm...."

"Hard drive...," he whispered, running his tongue along the curve of her ear.

"Mmm...keep going."

"Firmware...." His hand slipped lower and cupped her breast.

Her hand cupped his groin at the same time. "Firm...yes." The Imperial March resonated through the room and interrupted their exchange. Cassandra pulled back and gave Trevor a droll look. "Really? For our doorbell?"

A boyish grin played on his lips. "What? It's perfect." His grin turned into a puzzled frown. "Who the fuck could be at the door? Only Stephan knows we are in Dublin. I don't think he gets back from California until sometime tomorrow. He couldn't get a flight out of San Francisco any earlier. Whoever it is, they have the worst timing ever."

"Dunno, but we better answer. It could be work related."

Trevor hung his head. "Fine." He sighed. "We'll continue our explorations of all things geek later, *a bhean*." He grinned and ran downstairs to answer the door.

Cassandra followed Trevor with her eyes as he disappeared from sight. He never ceased to amaze and amuse her. She shook her head but couldn't shake the feeling that there was something strange going on. At times, she had caught a suspiciously secretive look on his face, but he hadn't said anything. Considering that the man couldn't keep a secret from her to save his life, she was probably imagining things due to the stress of the last month filled with wedding preparations.

They still had so much to do to get things rolling smoothly at their new house. A home they could comfortably grow into together. They would create many memories within those walls, and she would cherish every single one of them. The novelty of their relationship and how she and Trevor had come to be still made her heart race; old fears still surfaced from time to time, but with each day, Trevor taught her new lessons on living life to the fullest, and she was an eager pupil, ready to absorb all he had to teach.

She picked up her bag and headed upstairs to check out the rest of the house. Excitement rippled through her and a smile bloomed on her face at the raw potential of the wide rooms and blank walls. First, she peeked into the office and loved the back-to-back light wood desks with enough workspace for the many desk organizers and notepads she planned on purchasing. The room was decked out with wall-to-wall cabinets filled with office paraphernalia: printers, copier, and fax machine all available within the airy space. Each desk had a neat dual-screen set up, and a flat-screen TV graced the back wall. Definitely Trevor's domain.

Moving across the hall to the master bedroom, which faced the front of the house, Cassandra stopped in her tracks. Seeing all their ideas and even the smallest request put together so flawlessly made her warm inside. The spacious room with its soothing palette—olive greens and browns—made for the perfect refuge. The built-in bookcases surrounding the hidden entertainment unit waited for books to fill them. A door off to the right from the entrance to the room led to the master bath. The front wall's double windows, encased by olive-beige drapes and sheers, offered a wide view of the park, an added bonus. Butterflies tickled her stomach when her eyes travelled the expanse of the king-size bed, which held a prominent place in the space, with in-wall nightstands gracing each side. An elegant chandelier immediately above the wide bed completed the romantic look she was aiming for when she had picked it for their bedroom while still in California. She could barely wait until she and Trevor could explore the room's wonders later.

★ ★ ★ ★ ★

Trevor descended the stairs to the foyer at a fast clip. He planned on getting the door business taken care of at warp speed so he could return to wooing his wife. Smiling widely, he opened the door to find a courier, who eyed him suspiciously. The man handed him a thick envelope and, with a glimpse at the sender's name, Trevor realized he was lucky to have answered the door. If Cassandra had received the envelope, it would have spoiled the plans he had for the upcoming weekend. His bride thought she was the ace in organization and itineraries. He would prove to her that he was just as good—with a little bit of help. She was in for a big surprise.

Chapter Three

The Kidnapping

T REVOR WAS UP TO SOMETHING. The days since their arrival had been spent in a shopping frenzy. Although they had all the time in the world to get things done, Cassandra had been anxious to get started. The groceries and office organization items that were at the top of her list had made Trevor groan. Their first real big purchase together as a couple, aside from the house, was a car. They had placed their order through Stephan after they had selected one that matched both their wish lists: hers a comfortable ride with lots of space in the trunk and a high safety rating; Trevor's, a big-ass stereo. She rolled her eyes. The thumping of the high bass could quite possibly be heard all the way to San Francisco as he chauffeured her around the city. A city he knew like the back of his hand, even after having spent many years away.

Even with all the distractions and the focus on the list of things they needed to tackle, she could still feel something was awry. She had caught Trevor's mischievous eyes on her time and again and her curiosity had been piqued to a bursting point—it was driving her nuts. Cassandra needed to find out what he was hiding, even if she had to find other means to coax the information out of him. She hadn't survived the farm without learning a trick or two.

Trevor sat at his computer and patiently watched as Cassandra puttered around the house and office for hours. She had mentioned she was going to pick up more groceries and stop at her favorite café on Grafton Street, but she hadn't budged yet. She moved things around and tinkered with pictures until he had thought she would never leave—almost as if she knew he was up to something.

"Have you looked at the post office box options?" He introduced the subject again, eyes glued to the screen as he scrolled through files George had sent him overnight. He hoped to divert her attention and maybe find a way to get her out of the house so he could put his plan in motion.

She stopped dead in her tracks. Cassandra liked to be prepared for everything. "Not yet. Why? Did George say something about it?"

She bit the bait and Trevor took it to the next level. "I believe we'll need that set up." He didn't need to mention it wasn't needed right that very moment.

"Oh. Okay then. I can handle that. I already have the location. I just have to hand in the payment and application form I filled out yesterday at the closest local Delivery Services Unit."

"When will you be doing that?" *Please say now.*

"I was going for a cup of coffee later. Might as well leave now and kill two birds with one stone."

He avoided looking at her, knowing he'd give himself away if he did. "Need company?" *No, no, no,* he chanted in his head.

"Nah. You seem to be busy. I can manage." He almost sighed in relief, but kept a straight face as she grabbed a few sheets of paper from her desk and headed to the door. "Need anything from the store?"

"Nope. Thanks. Taking the car?" Again, he hoped she would make things easy on him and walk the short distance to the Delivery Center.

"Not until I get the lay of the land. It won't be long, though. It's a nice day out. I might as well enjoy it before the cold days arrive."

"True. Taking your phone?"

"Yes, Dad."

"Hey! The only time that word is used is when I ask you 'who's your Daddy.'"

"Funny boy…. Behave! I should be back in an hour or so."

The minute she walked out, Trevor ran from the office to their bedroom window and held his breath as he followed her across the street until she disappeared around the corner. He chuckled as he retrieved the duffel bags from the closet and mumbled to himself, "Shite, I never do anything the easy way." He sat the duffels on the bed and began packing their things for the little getaway. It would have been easier if he could have handled all that the night before, but Cassandra would have sniffed out his little surprise in a New York minute.

Even though Cassandra didn't seem to care much about a formal honeymoon, as geeky as he was, his traditional side knew that it was a must-have and something she would cherish in the future. With the list that Máire had sent him, Trevor elected to stick to the emerald island and, with her help, had booked a getaway at the Waterside House Hotel in Dublin. The hotel had beautiful panoramic views of the northerly coastline.

Once it had been booked, Trevor found himself looking forward to their trip. He and Cassandra had not been to a hotel since their stay in Paris. Although that trip had brought them together, it had not been a romantic getaway. The thought of having her to himself under more romantic circumstances sent his pulse pounding a hard rhythm in his veins.

That weekend he was kidnapping her and whisking her away for a romantic honeymoon. Their room had come complete with a balcony overlooking the Irish Sea, dinner, full Irish breakfast, and horseback riding on the beach.

He shook his head and powered on. He'd gotten a little sidetracked with her collection of lacy panties and brassieres. Looking up and mouthing "Thank you," he dove into the strenuous task of selecting only a couple of the tantalizing swatches of temptation. More likely than not, they would last only a few seconds on her, but he would enjoy every single second of that view. He had taken a chance on a couple of eyebrow-raising pairs and had to catch his breath and rearrange himself at the thought of her in them.

★ ★ ★ ★ ★

An hour later, he had stuffed a few changes of clothes, a few more undergarments than she would need for the two-night stay, and swimsuits for them both. With clothes handled, he added his shaving kit to his bag then returned to the bathroom for her toiletries. He opened drawers, looking for items he thought Cassandra would need, aside from a toothbrush. Exasperated, he ran his hand thought his hair. *What the hell?* There were more doodads, sticks, pencils, brushes, and balms than a full-fledged computer toolkit had screws and cables.

At a loss, he shrugged and started tossing bottles in a zip bag, and grabbed her blow dryer for good measure. He'd seen her use that regularly, even though he preferred the wild look her hair took when it dried naturally. *I'll make sure she has no time to think about blow-drying anything.* The wicked thought crossed his mind and made him smile. Back at the bed, he dropped them in her duffel, zipped it and, with both bags in hands, hurried down the two flights of stairs to the foyer.

Trevor knew he was cutting it close and a rush of adrenaline buzzed his veins, revving him into gear. He locked up and headed to their parking space at the back of the house to get their new sedan. Tossing the bags in the back seat, he slid behind the wheel and drove around to the front of the house just as Cassandra rounded the corner. With her nose buried in a document, she never looked up when he honked the horn and pushed open the passenger door.

When he honked the horn a third time, her chest heaved and she exploded. "Listen buddy, you can take your horn and shove—Trevor? What the hell?" Cassandra's bewildered expression changed to a frown when her eyes locked on the car.

"Hey pretty lass, are you always this feisty?" He asked with an eyebrow-waggle. "Need a ride?"

The frown deepened and Cassandra narrowed her eyes. "What's with the car? Going somewhere?"

Trevor laughed and waved her over. "Jump in."

She shook her head. A puzzled smile curved her lips as she slid into the passenger seat. She glanced in the back and her eyes snared his, studying him with a curious intensity. "Bags?"

Her suspicious tone tickled his fancy. Damn. He loved stumping her. "Yep."

"And you packed them yourself?"

"Yep."

"Wow. Surprisingly efficient." She grinned, looking around the car and out the window. "And where did you say my husband is tucked?"

"What? I can plan stuff, you know," Trevor pouted jokingly.

Cassandra grinned cheekily at him. "Uh, yeah. And who taught you that skill?!" Her hand dropped to his thigh and she patted it soothingly. "Gonna share details?"

"Nope. Surprise. You'll see once we're there." A curious glint flowed into her eyes and a soft smile curved her lips. He could tell she was dying to ask questions, but she bit her lip. His grin grew wider when his inquisitive twenty-question wife settled back against her seat, determined to hold her tongue.

"Don't worry, love. It's only a kidnapping." He took her hand in his and brought it to his lips as he pulled into traffic. "Relax. We have about a short drive ahead of us."

"If you say so." By Cassandra's tone, Trevor knew her mind was running a mile a minute. No itinerary. No details. She was probably churning up inside. Damn, he loved her.

Turning east, they ran into the typical Friday afternoon traffic. He flashed her quick smile. "Once we clear traffic, it should only take us about twenty minutes to get to where we are going." He returned his eyes to the road ahead, a grin plastered on his face. For once—just once—he'd stumped the master.

Trevor gave himself a high five in his head for a job well done and he made a mental note to send Máire flowers upon their return. The rest of the drive took place in a comfortable silence. Reaching his exit, he pulled off and headed in the direction of the hotel.

As they neared the waterfront, Cassandra sat higher in her seat and leaned toward the windshield in anticipation as a beautiful building came into view. Ever since finding him grinning at her from the car, her heart had been pounding in her chest. The pressure hadn't eased as the car ate up the miles. His glances and touches had added to the mix, leaving her skin tingling and a tight sensation in the pit of her stomach.

They had not truly had quality time together without preparations for the move and work butting in since their return from Paris. Yes, they had their home; however, this was their first real road trip as a married couple. Anticipation held her in its tight grip and she had to clasp her hands in her lap.

She grinned inside. You'd think it was their first time alone together the way her hands trembled. The internal grin faded and her mouth went dry on remembering that first night in Paris. That first night they.... Cassandra could feel the heat rising up her neck and had an overwhelming urge to fan herself. *Get a grip. Jeez.*

Pulling into the parking lot, Trevor cut the engine and turned in his seat to face her. "*So, a ghrá.* What do you think?"

Cassandra was awed by the fact that Trevor had snuck one by her. Stunned really, not because he wasn't capable, but because whenever he tried to be sneaky, he could never hold it in. In the couple of months before their wedding, she had caught him red-handed a few times, planning small surprises that never came to fruition. This time, not even a peep. A huge smile spread on her face. "It's beautiful!"

Trevor grinned and nodded in the direction of the hotel. "Shall we check it out?"

"Hell, yeah!" She laughed and hopped out of the car, grabbing one of the bags from the back seat. Trevor grabbed the other and walked around the car to join her. As she watched him approach, her eyes widened and her jaw almost hit the pavement. "Where's Jack II? Where the hell is Jill? No laptops? You never travel without him."

"As much as it pains me to say this, Jack and Jill are at home. This is our time. No work. Just fun. Stephan and George know how to reach us." He crossed his heart with a finger. "I promise you'll be front and center in my thoughts at all times, *a ghrá*."

A slow burn set off inside Cassandra at hearing his words. She was looking forward to that promise becoming a reality. Taking her hand, he led the way to the front desk.

While Trevor checked them in, Cassandra moved to the window and looked out at the deep blue sea. The waves rolled toward the shore in a tumble of white foaming caps. The scenery reminded her of the San Francisco Bay but wilder, untamed, powered by the mystical history of the land.

"Ready?" Trevor's lips were close by her ear and his tone was low, wicked.

Her heart pounded hard and fast in expectation of what was to come. "Ready and willing."

As they walked up the stairs to the second floor, Trevor ran his hand along the curve of Cassandra's waist, settling it familiarly there. "What do you think, Cassie girl? Nice place?"

"Yet to be seen, geek. Depends on the adventure and," she looked him over, "the ride."

Trevor burst out in a deep throaty laugh that carried the assurance of sinful deeds to come. She shivered at the twinge of expectancy that hit her lower tummy. As they arrived at the door to their room, he gave her the run-down. "Okay. For your viewing pleasure, and no...I'm not talking about me...well, at least not yet, we have the Honeymoon Suite with a balcony overlooking the Irish Sea. From the balcony, you can see Ireland's Eye and Howth Head along the coastline."

A slight smile curved Cassandra's lips as she plucked the key from his fingers and pushed open the door. Trevor followed her, continuing with his recital of the details. "Tomorrow, after a full hearty Irish breakfast, we have a reservation to go horseback riding."

She raised an eyebrow. "An Irishman on a horse." She cocked her head and appraised his long lean, muscular body. "Will you be wearing a kilt?"

His eyes narrowed. "Uh, no. The boys don't want to be bouncing in the wind."

A giggle burst from her mouth and she eyed the room decorated in creams and dark woods. A large, old-style wooden four-poster bed was centered along the main wall of the room and was flanked by matching nightstands. A desk and small chest of drawers were situated on the wall facing the bed, and a large glass window and sliding glass doors opened onto a balcony. Cassandra moved to the bed and tested it with her hand. "Nice soft bed, hearty Irish breakfast, horseback riding, and the Irish sea. Did I say nice soft bed?"

A smile quirked his mouth as he too eyed the bed, and heat flared in his eyes. He took a step toward her. "Yes, *a ghrá*. You mentioned the bed already."

Swallowing hard, she set her bag on the floor and walked around the bed to the huge sliding doors overlooking the sea to compose herself. The day was sunny and warm for September. She slid the door open and a soft breeze blew from the sea, taking the edge off the heat of the sun and from her cheeks.

The view of the vast beach, perfect for long walks, begged for some alone time. Her heart raced as Trevor approached her, wrapped his arms around her waist, and pulled her back against his chest. He dropped a kiss on the top of her head. "It's beautiful, Trevor."

Trevor chuckled. "Good enough for a surprise honeymoon?" His hands gripped her hips and turned her to face him. "I know you said it could wait, but I wanted it to be now. Before things get even crazier, I just wanted some time alone with you. No phones ringing. No conference calls or couriers coming to the door. Just us, pampering and loving each other to the fullest."

"I know what you mean. We've been so wrapped up in the wedding, your new assignment with the NSA, and the move that we've barely been able to breathe." She cupped his face with her hands and stood on tippy toes. "I am glad you kidnapped me, Mr. Brennan." Her use of his real name always enveloped him in deep pleasure. It was a small secret only a few people knew about and that he and Cassandra cherished as a treasure. "And to think I was going to send you packing." Cassandra pressed her lips to his and sighed as she wrapped her arms around him, squeezing him tight. "I need time with you, too. The idea of having you all to myself is pretty sexy. Now, stop talking and kiss me."

Her soft demand sent a jolt of lust straight to his cock and he complied immediately, taking her mouth in a deep wet kiss. Her body sank into his, her hands slid under his shirt, sending a shiver up his spine. He nipped her bottom lip with his teeth and pulled back, holding her as they remained locked in a half embrace, panting and shaking.

"Damn, Trevor. That kiss…definitely the death of me."

Trevor wiggled his eyebrows. "Kiss of Death, huh?"

Her eyes gleamed. "Oh, yeah. Deadly."

He breathed in the fresh salty air blowing in the room from the sea. "It's a beautiful day. As much as I'd love to jump your bones right this minute, the sun is too nice to pass up. Soon the winter will be here and we'll be freezing our asses. Let's go for a walk." Cassandra laughed as he herded her to the door. "Time to play lizards, Cassie girl. Soak up the sun."

Cassandra accepted his hand as he led her out the door and toward the path to the beach. When they reached the soft sand, they slipped off their shoes. Cassandra giggled as she sank her feet in the sand and wiggled her toes. The sheer pleasure mirrored on her face brought amusement and a sense of accomplishment to his heart. "Come on!" She tugged on his hand, pulling him to the edge of the water. Gentle waves licked the sand and rolled over their feet, chilling them, but the warm sun rays eased the chill as the waves receded.

Trevor inhaled a big draught of air. The scent of the sea—a mix of salty water and seaweed—dragged long-buried memories from their confines. Memories of his hometown, Sligo, which also lay by the sea, sunny days spent at the beach in Drumcliff and Rosses Point as a youngster tumbled over like the rolling waves on the beach. On impulse, he brought Cassandra's hand to his lips and pressed a hard kiss against it. "Thank you."

She squinted in the bright sun at him. "For...?"

"For putting up with me. I can be an ass and forget about things sometimes. I should have arranged for this to happen the day we flew in." Squeezing her hand, he looked down into her eyes, hoping the emotions churning inside him would speak of how much he loved her. That she was part of his soul.

The serious expression gleaming from his beautiful blue eyes tugged at her heart and it skipped a beat. It was moments like those that left her wondering what her life would have been like if her father hadn't assigned the Bristol account to her, if Allison hadn't taken the trial results and formula, and if Trevor's curiosity hadn't driven him to check out the server when he did. Deep down, she knew. She didn't need to wonder.

Cassandra squeezed his hand and shot him a saucy grin. "I know that there is not a single day either of us forgets who we are to each other. Let's just enjoy this moment." She stepped into him and pulled his face to hers, kissing him softly on the lips. She smiled against them as she squeezed his ass cheek. "For the record, you have a mighty fine ass, Mr. Brennan."

He chuckled and reciprocated with a little slap to hers as they began their trek down the beach. When they came across a nice grassy area at the foot of the round tower bordering the hotel's property, Cassandra detoured to the patch. She sat facing the water and Trevor scooted behind her, settling her between his thighs. She leaned back against his chest with a content sigh.

Cradling her in his arms, he rested his chin on her head and enjoyed the sight and sounds around them—the warmth of the sun on their skin, the crashing waves on the beach, the fine mist kissing their faces, the seagulls flying above them. All of it made for a peaceful, grounding experience. Their first time away from everything and everybody, away from work.

Lifting his face to the sun, Trevor enjoyed the press of Cassandra's body against his. As the sounds of life in motion flooded his senses, he let his mind travel back to a few months ago. It felt like ages away, and yet it hadn't been that long ago that Cassandra had spun his world on its axis. Since that day it seemed as if she had always been a part of him, always been at his side. Cassandra's hair caressed his arm as the cool fingers of the sea breeze blew the silky stray wisps.

The urge to kiss her overwhelmed him and he cupped her face, turning it to him. Leaning down, he pressed his lips to her fuller softer ones. The wetness of her tongue running along his lower lip, licking the corner of his mouth teasingly and nipping it with her teeth, sent a spear of electrical heat straight to his groin. With a groan, he pulled her snug against him, plunging his tongue deep into her mouth, exploring its sweet velvety softness, scraping against her teeth, and tangling with her tongue. Cassandra turned sideways and looped an arm around his neck, rubbing her breasts against his chest.

Her pebbled nipples were visible through her thin knit shirt. "Cassie…" he moaned against her mouth, deepening the kiss and rolling them on the small patch of grass and sand. He covered her with his body and slid a leg between her knees. His thigh pressed and rubbed against the warmth of her sex through the fabric of her Capri pants. Her heated response made him want to throw caution to the wind and pretend they were not in a public area. He settled for kissing her deeper. For now.

Trevor's firm and demanding mouth sent a spear of desire from her breast straight to her clit, which throbbed with each little touch of his thigh. Running her hand from his thigh to his hip, her fingers dug deep and fisted his jeans covering his ass, pulling him tighter against her.

Dropping her head back, she sucked in shaky gasps of air. "Never enough. I can't get enough of you," she whispered against his lips as she adjusted her body and rocked her hips against the ridge of his hard erection. Trevor captured her mouth again, sucking on her lips as he slipped a hand under her shirt, pushing it up her stomach. The breeze blew goose bumps across her exposed skin and she moaned at the sensation.

As his hand cupped her breast, the goose bumps turned to a shiver. His fingers played her, kneading her breast and flicking her nipple through the lace. Her breath hitched with each brush across the sensitive flesh, which, addicted to his touch, responded to his ministrations avidly, pebbling and tightening.

"Oh Trevor, yes," she exhaled, breaking the kiss and arching her back, forcing more of her breast into his hand.

"God, I love how your body responds to me." he murmured against her ear, skimming his lips along the line of her jaw to her neck, leaving a trail of kisses down to the valley of her breasts. Cupping the back of his neck, Cassandra's body shuddered when his hot, moist mouth took her nipple and sucked it, nipped it over her shirt.

"God, Cassie I need to taste your skin," he groaned against her chest as he slowly slid his hand back down along her side and then reversed the motion, pushing her shirt up further to give him the access he craved.

Oblivious to their surroundings, Trevor admired her breasts under the sexy lacy bra. The white see-through material contrasted with her golden skin and gave him a glimpse of the tight dusky nipples underneath. His cock twitched and his throat grew as dry as the Sahara. Reverently, he uncovered a turgid breast and pebbled nipple to his touch and mouth. Sucking it deep, he traced circles around the erect nipple with his tongue, flicking it with each groan of her pleasure. Her warm salty taste on his tongue, enhanced by her little gasps, was killing him.

He rubbed his thigh against Cassandra's sex and she instinctively rocked her hips against it in the same slow cadence, moaning softly with each hard grind. "I want you," he breathed out harshly, resting his forehead against the valley between her breasts. "But not here...we could get busted any moment. I have no control where you are concerned." Cassandra cupped his face and tipped it to look into her eyes.

"I know, love. I want you too. If we don't stop now we might get arrested for indecent exposure." A giggle bubbled up and burst from her lips. "Oh my god. I can see oh-so-proper Stephan's face when he gets the call to bail us out." Trevor guffawed and rolled to his side next to her on the grassy knoll. He lay beside her, watching the sparse clouds float across the crisp blue sky while they composed themselves, waiting for their breathing and hearts to regain their regular rhythm.

All Cassandra could focus on was Trevor lying next to her and how just a little look from him could melt her on the spot. *Oh man, if Jessie could see me now she'd be laughing her ass off singing, "Na-Na-Na-Na-Na-Na."* The wind carried the sound of voices to them and snapped them out of their sensual haze.

A chill crept across her skin when Trevor pulled back from her abruptly. Laughing out loud, she scrambled to fix her bra and readjust her shirt as she sat up. She felt like teenager on the verge of being caught kissing a boy. Trevor's laughter joined hers as he quickly adjusted himself. She leaned over and kissed him hard on the lips. "We reined it in just in the nick of time."

At that moment, a family of four appeared on the path in front of them. "Shite!" Trevor cursed under his breath as he sat up and tried to disguise the tent action in his pants. The man nodded to them and Trevor returned the greeting. Once the small group was far enough along the beach, Trevor and Cassandra burst out laughing. Standing, they brushed the evidence of their little romp on the beach from their clothes and made their way back to the hotel under the setting sun.

Chapter Four

No Boundaries

TREVOR LEANED AGAINST THE BEDPOST, flipping through a magazine while waiting for Cassandra to finish getting ready for dinner. Their plans were to eat at the luxurious restaurant in the hotel. His thoughts were focused on his new bride. Why she was taking so long was beyond him. As far as he was concerned, she was stunning without the need for makeup and whatnots.

As if on cue, Cassandra strode out of the bathroom, wearing a gold brocade strappy dress that flowed to her thighs. The front of the dress plunged for miles it seemed, and displayed the creamy curves and valley of her breasts. Trevor's breath stalled in his chest and his brain seized. One thought echoed clearly. *That's my wife. My woman.* "You look amazing," he managed to blurt out as he stood, feeling like a teenager on a first date.

"Why thank you, sir." A wicked smile played at the corner of her lips and his heart did another flip. "For a geek, you clean up nice and shiny yourself," she chuckled and moved to the bed to grab her wrap. Swinging it over her bare shoulders, she approached him. With a hand resting on her lower back, Trevor led her from the room and toward their dinner date.

As Cassandra walked beside Trevor, all she could focus on was the warmth of his hand at the small of her back. The heat of it branding her with a stamp of possession she found strangely appealing. She slanted a glance at him from the corner of her eye, ogling the way his slacks tightened around his thighs as he walked and how the white button-up shirt brought out the striking dark blue of his eyes. Her heart raced at the fantasy of her hands pushing the shirt from his shoulders. She chuckled to herself and shook her head. *Damn, I'm in so much trouble.*

Trevor delighted himself throughout the evening with the vision of a laughing and smiling Cassandra. Dinner went off without a hitch; the food was tasty, the wine delicious, the atmosphere perfect for a romantic getaway, just like he had envisioned for them. They spent the next few hours enjoying each other's company, talking about trivial things, which somehow felt important and precious because they were covering new territory. There was so much still left to be shared—but they had a whole life ahead of them to indulge in a slow discovery.

After the waiter cleared the table, Trevor leaned forward and took Cassandra's hand in his as they continued their exchange. "…I kid you not. I locked myself out of the hotel room in my pajamas in New York during one of our operations. Nate has never let me live that one down."

Trevor laughed at the mental image, then frowned a bit at the thought that Nelson had been there with her. "Why don't we take this upstairs? I want to be alone with my wife…." Her eyes flared hot, reflecting his own need and, with that one look, they both knew that night would be a night of no-reservations loving. No boundaries, no hesitation. Nothing to come between them. Trevor tugged her to her feet and guided her to the bank of elevators. They rode up to their floor as he continued to caress her hand in sensual strokes along her palm and wrist.

Cassandra's thoughts narrowed to every little caress sending electric shocks through her system; by the time they stopped at their floor her heart was racing a mile a minute, reminding her of another thrilling elevator ride. It was always like the first time—the anticipation, breathlessness, and need.

When the elevator slid open, Trevor led the way to their door. Cassandra stepped into the room with him close on her heels. His nearness kindled a hot windstorm of fire that had burned low in her belly since their earlier tryst on the beach.

"Would you like a glass of wi—?" The question died on her lips when she caught the gleam in his eyes and watched, mesmerized, as his tongue slipped between his lips, moistening them. *Damn sexy.* Her body swayed toward his and their lips came together in a hot, wet kiss.

Their tongues danced together, gliding, tasting, exploring. At times going deep, harder, and others soft, gentle. Teeth lightly pulling at each other's lips, playing with the corners of their mouths before diving deep again. Hands joined in the exploration—Cassandra's slid up under his shirt following the muscles and ridges of his back, and his eased to the small of hers.

Trevor molded her body against him, her contours melting perfectly into his. She moaned and ground against the ridge of his shaft trapped between them. He wanted to take her, bury himself deep inside her warmth. But first, he wanted to hear her moans of pleasure as he relished the taste of her exploding on his tongue. Feel her soft flesh contracting around his fingers and, finally, enjoy the fruits of his labors when she screamed his name in ecstasy.

Cupping her face with his hands, he deepened the kiss and groaned as her hands gripped his ass, pulling him snug against her groin and grinding against him. "*A ghrá,* slow down. We have all the time in the world. Let me take you slow. I want you to come in my mouth before I fill you."

She moaned and replied in a raspy tone, "Yes…please."

Trevor took Cassandra by the hand, backing toward the bed, and when the edge hit his legs, he sat, pulling her closer to stand between his thighs.

The sight of the silky confection, such a contrast to the jeans and tee shirts she typically wore, made his cock swell. He slid the straps of her dress off her shoulders and her arms reached back and eased the zipper down. He pushed the dress over her hips, allowing the soft silky fabric to fall carelessly to the floor at her feet.

He leaned forward and walked a finger across the top of the lacey cups of her bra, trailing his nail across the smooth skin of her curves. With each brush of his finger, her nipples puckered until they were tight little buds straining against the material. Her head rolled back and a soft sigh passed from her lips when he brushed his palms over them before tugging the now offending lace down to reveal her darkened rosy peaks.

Trevor's pulse raced and he all but drooled, wanting to feel her soft flesh in his mouth. He leaned forward as he stroked her breasts, cupping them, raising the turgid nipples to his mouth. He teased her, rubbing the tight buds with his lips, blowing moist hot air across them.

Cassandra moaned, combing her fingers through his hair, holding him in place. Her hips jerked when his mouth wrapped around her nipple and sucked it deep into his mouth, pulling and tugging on it with his teeth, twirling it with his tongue. Splaying his hands on her back, he pulled her in even closer. The scent of her sensual sweet musky arousal filled the air and he wanted more.

Each pull of his mouth on her breast and swirl of his tongue sent a bolt of heat straight to Cassandra's pulsing clit, swollen from the teasing of the day and the little touches here and there. Moaning deep in her throat, her fingers clutched at his hair and her body arched, aching for him to take more. His hands slid from her back to her hips and held them prisoner between his legs.

Her body shuddered and her knees grew weak as he trailed kisses to her other breast. The graze of his teeth across the sensitive nipple sent an arrow of heat deep in her tummy, and when he bit down gently she cried out, "Trevor! Yes, like that. So good. God, your mouth...so hot...."

Her heart tripped in her chest, her pulse a loud beat in her ears as his hands glided down her legs, pausing to stroke the sensitive skin behind her knees before moving up the inside of her thighs. When his lips pressed against the supple sensitive skin of her abdomen, her muscles jumped and another wave of need struck her pulsing clit. Wanting to give as good as she got, she stepped back and, fastening her eyes on his, kneeled in front of him.

The bulge of his cock straining against the fabric of his slacks brought a soft smile to the corner of her lips. He sucked in a long breath as her hands began a slow journey from his knees to his groin; her thumbs brushed along the inside of his thighs, then gently teased his hard erection. Trevor's low groan filled the room. "Cassie girl, come onto the bed."

"In a moment," she whispered softly and reached for the button of his slacks, loosening it and pulling the sides apart, forcing his zipper down. "God. Love it when you go commando. Makes life so much more interesting." Trevor's chuckle merged into a sharp intake of breath when she pushed his trousers further apart, easing his cock and balls from their confining space. "Can a woman call a man's cock lovely?" she asked, tracing a finger down the prominent vein, making his cock dance under her feather touch. Cassandra hummed low in her voice when his shaft pulsed and surged under her fingertips, leaving him hard and ready. She wanted to tease him as he had teased her. "You always say 'payback,' right?"

"Shite, Cassandra. Move your ass to the bed."

His demanding gaze riveted her on the spot and she wanted to comply with his wish. A delightful shiver of wanting ran through her and she shook her head. "Soon. Busy here," she whispered. She gripped the edges of his pants and tugged until he lifted his ass to help her pull them off his hips, down his legs and out of her way. She coaxed him to the edge of the bed, settling between his spread thighs.

Her own breath grew shallow and a surge of moisture coated her folds when she leaned in, brushed her lips across his silky crown, flicking her tongue and lapping up the tangy drop of pre-come pooling at the engorged tip. Trevor groaned and his hips jerked. His hand buried itself in her silky hair and tightened as her hand brushed up his thigh, gripped the base of his cock, and brought it to her lips again, spreading his salty essence over them.

She ran her wet tongue around the sensitive ridge of nerves along the underside of his crown and followed the path her fingers had taken, licking along the pulsing vein to his balls. She continued her sampling, trailing her tongue across the smooth skin from the tip to base, nipping on the tender flesh separating his tight balls. The warm earthy scent of his skin sent another wave of heat rolling through her.

Cassandra moaned softly and reached her tongue out again, licking her way back to his pulsing crown. She wrapped her lips around his glistening head and sucked hard. His hips jumped and his fingers fisted her hair tighter as she suckled him, pulling him deeper, swallowing him. Trevor's hiss was music to her ears as she flicked her tongue around his hard length, laving, pulling back, and swallowing him deep again. He arched his hips and ground against her lips, his tempo matching each stroke of her mouth, each flick of her tongue.

"Cassie girl," Trevor growled and tried to pull out. "Stop! If you keep that up I won't last." Cassandra shook her head and gripped his hips, holding him in place. As she continued to stroke him with her mouth, she reached down and rolled his balls in her hand, squeezing them gently.

"Fuck!" he breathed out in a harsh burst of air and fell back on the bed as his balls tightened and his cock grew even harder.

His heart stopped and his lungs froze when her hand wrapped around the base of his shaft, trapping his balls tight against its length. Her hot tongue scorched him each time she sucked him to the hilt and swiped her tongue across the top of his captured sac. A tingling flared from his lower back to his toes and his back arched from the bed when her teeth grazed his length and she suckled his engorged head.

"Cassandra!" His yell rang through the room, and yet she wanted more from him.

She relaxed her throat, tightened her fingers around his shaft, and took him even deeper, pumping him in and out of her mouth. Trevor's curses combined with Irish endearments she'd come to know well crowded the air, his hips thrust against her mouth, quickening. She groaned when her tongue felt a pulse flood along the vein of his shaft, and she almost came when his back lifted from the bed as he yelled her name again. Her inner muscles clenched and her clit throbbed when the first rush of his seed hit the back of her throat. Her hands gripped his trembling hips and her mouth continued to pull on his pulsing cock, sucking, swallowing, and milking him dry until he collapsed back on the bed.

"Shite! Cassie."

With slow deliberation, Cassandra released his semi-soft shaft and trailed kisses along his inner thigh until she stood on her knees between his legs. She watched the rise and fall of his chest, which matched her laboring lungs, and she grinned wickedly as she brushed the tips of her fingers along his jerky stomach muscles. Trevor dropped his chin to his chest and gazed down the length of his body at her. A gleam flared bright within their depths when he caught her smile.

Chapter Five

Busy Here

HE SAT ABRUPTLY, GRIPPED HER by the elbows, and brought her up with him as he stood. Turning, he tossed her back on the bed and followed her down, trapping her with his arms and legs, capturing her mouth in a searing kiss. The length of his lean muscular body scorched her, sending a rush of molten lava deep in her belly. Her abdominal muscles flexed and her inner muscles pulsed with each stroke of his tongue. She opened her mouth to him and explored his in turn, sucking his tongue into her mouth, using the same suction she'd used on his cock.

Breaking the kiss, Trevor sat back on his heels. "You cheated. I told you. We're taking this slow. Now, it's my turn." Grabbing her by the waist, he gently pulled her to the center of the bed and kneeled beside her. He gazed on her body resting languorously on the wide bed. A deep rumble vibrated in his chest. The caveman in him rejoiced to finally have her under his control, soon to be under him as he took her the way he wanted. "You're so beautiful, Cassie...." Trevor quickly chucked his shirt, spread her legs, and, supporting his weight on his elbows, made himself comfortable between her silky thighs.

His fingers slid along the full length of her, massaging the already flowing juices along her folds. Spreading her gently and exposing her sensitive bud with his thumbs, he took his first taste and moaned at her heady essence. "Fuck, Cassie. You taste good." A small moan escaped her in a raspy breath and her eyes closed in pleasure. He intended to give her more with the use of his mouth, tongue, and fingers until she begged to be taken, begged for his weight to blanket her. "How do you want it, babe? Tell me." His tone was hoarse and he could barely restrain his own need, but before he allowed himself to plunge into her heat, he wanted to make her come.

Lying on the bed, spread before Trevor, the only thoughts swirling in Cassandra's head were how much she had wanted this all day. The feel of his warm breath against her clit caused her stomach muscles to tighten in anticipation. "Trevor! I just want you. Whatever you want," she whispered into the quiet of the room, stretching her arms above her head and arching her back off the bed, feeling wanton and beautiful under his gaze.

A low rumble came from Trevor's throat and reverberated against her sex as his mouth covered her, sucking her deep. Flicking his tongue along her slick folds, he teased her by circling her clit with his tongue without actually touching it. He groaned as her hips bucked against him, needing him to put her out of her misery and capture that tiny bundle of sensitive nerves with his lips. But he ignored her urging and continued his slow torture, exploring every inch, stroking and lapping at the juices flowing solely for him.

His fingers slid from her folds and travelled over her hips to grip her ass cheeks. Lifting them, he buried his face deeper, still teasing his tongue along her slit and around her clit before stabbing it deep into her channel, thrusting in and out repeatedly, his actions a promise of more to come.

Cassandra's thighs trembled and her stomach clenched as he continued his assault, slowly licking his way back to the one spot she craved for him to touch. A rush of blood went straight to her head. She shifted her hips restlessly and cried out, "Trevor! Please!"

He licked a path around the outer edge of her sex to the juncture of her hip. She fisted his hair, and held him to her as her hips, no longer under her control, thrust against his face, seeking his mouth. She burned inside with the need for him to claim her. "Goddamn it Trevor! Stop fucking around. Just take me already!"

Lifting his head, Trevor's eyes gleamed wickedly from under half-closed lids. "Soon. Busy here." He dropped his head back between her thighs.

Cassandra's chuckle transformed into a soft "Oh" as he finally took her clit between his teeth and quickly flicked his tongue across it. Her back bowed off the bed again and her hands flung out, fisting the covers. With each swipe of his tongue across her tight bundle of nerves, a little jolt of electricity shot through her body, from her chest down to her womb. Her heart rose to her throat and her breath stalled when his fingers pinched and rolled her nipple. His mouth was relentless and Cassandra soared on the edge of a rising tide of pleasure. Her hips began to piston against the pull of his lips. Blood roared in her ears, her body tensed and shook out of control as she approached her release. "Ah…Trevor…So close, babe… so close."

Trevor reveled in her quaking under his hands and mouth. He slid his other hand from her ass to her folds, trailing his fingers down her wet hot slit, and sank two fingers deep inside her as he continued to suck on her swollen nub. Her hips jerked and her breath hitched as she bore down on his hand. He broke the intimate kiss solely to gaze on her glistening, rosy, plump flesh as he continued to thrust his fingers in and out of her. *All mine.* A quick glance at Cassandra sent a rush of lava-hot blood straight to his cock. Eyes closed, lips parted in abandon, she pinched and plucked her own nipples as she rocked her hips in sensual movements against his hand.

"Trevor…please…don't stop…." Her plea was a rush through his veins and his breathing accelerated as he dipped his fingers and spread her creamy arousal into her folds again, coating them. Her eyes snared his and darkened when he brought his slick fingers to his mouth and sucked her nectar off them.

"You taste like heaven, Cassandra." Without hesitation, he slid one finger and then a second back into her hot, silky channel.

"Yes…" she moaned.

Initiating a slow cadence, he watched as her hips synched to his rhythm, meeting his thrusts with upward swings. Soon her inner muscles tightened around him, indicating she floated on the edge of her release again. "Trevor!"

His cock grew heavy again with need and his mouth went dry as the first little spasms rippled around his fingers. He leaned in again and captured her clit in his mouth, alternating between flicking the sensitive tip with his tongue and sucking the fleshy nub deep in his mouth with just enough suction to drive her wild.

Within a few minutes, Cassandra's body clutched at his fingers and throbbed against his tongue as she exploded in her release. She quaked and shuddered under his mouth, drenching his fingers with her sweet arousal. He continued to pump in and out of her and suck her until she fell back against the bed in a boneless heap. He kissed the trembling muscle of her thigh, sporting a satisfied grin as he listened to her efforts to regain her breath.

"That was unbelievably good…but I need more…I need to feel you inside me." The hoarse tone of her voice brought his cock to full-on erection and it hardened almost to the point of pain.

"I need to be inside you, too," he murmured as he stretched over her, laying his weight on her welcoming body. He spread her thighs with his knee and nestled between them. His engorged head found her hot entrance and, with a slight rocking of his hips, he rubbed it against her slit in a tantalizing massage.

"Now, Trevor. I want you now."

He lunged and thrust deep, filling her to the hilt. They both moaned as her heat fully enveloped him. "Fuck," Trevor rasped out.

Cassandra pushed her feet against the bed, lifting her hips to meet each of his thrusts. Body tingling and lungs struggling for air, her hands cupped his face and she brought his lips closer to hers, whispering his name before plunging her tongue deep into his mouth.

She wrapped her legs around his hips, locking them at the ankles, pulling him closer with a press of her heels against his ass. As they continued to dance, their tongues caressed each other, twining and sliding. Feeling the heat build again deep inside, her legs tightened and her hands dropped to the bed, clutching the covers, her knuckles turning white. Her body arched into his and her inner muscles clenched, wanting to keep him deep inside, pulsing each time he pulled away. "Damn, Trevor. I feel every inch of you."

Her words burst the dam and he increased his rhythm to a faster cadence. Their moans and groans mingled with the slapping sounds of flesh against flesh, their bodies coated in a thin film of glistening sweat. Soon Trevor felt the sensations mounting and the tell-tale twinge at the base of his spine proclaiming his release closing in on him.

"Oh, Trevor...I'm coming...yes!"

Her inner muscles squeezed his shaft and all his control evaporated in a split second. "Cassandra!" He buried his face in the crook of her neck and his hands bunched up the sheets as he climaxed, his hips pistoning out of control. Her spasms milked him with each push, each withdrawal, until he was drained. Spent, he collapsed on her, breathing hard and heavy, trying his best not to crush her with his weight. In a last burst of energy, he rolled to the side, bringing her with him.

He held Cassandra against his length and she snuggled close, resting her head on his chest and tucking a leg between his. They simply held on to each other, riding out the last waves of their pleasure, waiting for their hearts and breathing to return to their normal rhythm.

With a content sigh, Cassandra kissed his shoulder. "You can do that to me forever if you like, my Lord. Will you, Trevor?" she breathed in a strong Scottish accent.

Trevor pressed his lips to her forehead and grinned. "Aye, blossom. I will."

She chuckled. "It never gets old. I love that quote from Highlander." She caressed Trevor's chest, resting her hand over the wild thumping of his heart. "I'm not kidding, you know. You can do that to me forever and it will never be enough, Trev." Her voice held a serious quality.

He cradled her in his arms and placed a soft kiss on the top of her head. "I know, Cassie. The feeling is mutual. I can't seem to get enough of you either. I don't see that ever happening." He reached for the covers and pulled them over their chilled bodies. They still had another full day at the hotel and he looked forward to spending it with her. He had no doubt it would be packed with fun. Leave it to Cassie to fill his life with joy, laughter, and love twenty-four seven. Feeling her body sink into his, Trevor gave in to exhaustion and slipped into a deep, sated sleep.

Epilogue

Restless

WAKING AND SITTING STRAIGHT UP, Cassandra pushed the hair from her face and glanced around the room. Something had woken her and she couldn't figure out what it was. Trevor's voice and the restless movements of his body under the covers broke the silence.

Leaning back on her elbow, she reached over and brushed his brow with her fingers. His dreams were holding him captive again and his muttering had pulled her from sleep. "Shush, Trevor. It's okay. I'm here." Her heart tumbled in her chest when he sighed her name and turned on his side, still deep in sleep.

Wide awake and restless, Cassandra eased back and slid from the bed. The room had a nip to it and a shiver shimmied up her spine. Rubbing at the goose bumps that peppered her arms, she snagged Trevor's shirt from the floor and slipped her arms into the sleeves as she moved to the window. Freeing her hair from the collar, she pushed back the curtain and looked out over the hotel grounds.

The Irish Sea was a dark blanket peppered with the glow of white foamy caps cresting the waves, crashing along the beach. The only light was from the distant polka dots of illumination shining from the wall sconces along the hotel's perimeter. Through the open sliding glass door, the smell of night—a mixture of wet earth and cool salty moist air—filled her senses.

This was the time of day, just before the sun's fingers crept on the horizon, that Cassandra loved best—a time where thoughts and dreams hovered. With a deep sigh, she rested her forehead against the cool, smooth windowpane and wrapped her arms around her body.

She wondered about the nature of Trevor's dream. She knew he was driven to find his parents, and there was no way she was letting him walk that path alone. If there was a chance, no matter how small, that they were out there, they would find them together. She would have felt the same way if her mother had been the one missing.

The thought of her mom sent a pang of pain straight through her heart. She had tried not to think of her these past weeks while planning for the wedding. Although it had been a long time since her mother's passing, Cassandra was certain she would have adored Trevor. Under all his geekiness was a gentle caring man who would have swept her mom off her feet, just as he had her.

The shifting of covers on the bed drew her attention and she turned, waiting to see if Trevor settled again. When he rolled to his back and the covers tangled with his legs, a smile quirked her lips. Damn, he was a force to be reckoned with. The man had stormed her walls like an army at the castle gates. She would do anything for him, something she had thought she would never feel for anyone.

Moving back to her side of the bed, she slipped his shirt off her shoulders and joined him under the covers. When the bed dipped under her weight, Trevor turned toward her and gathered her in his arms. His moist breath caressed her forehead and his soft sigh soothed her soul. Snuggling closer, she wrapped her arm around his waist and let his warmth seep into her skin.

A satisfied smile curved her lips as a last thought before reaching oblivion popped in her head. They had another day at the hotel, another day full of laughter, love, and ecstasy only Trevor knew how to give her—and she would be enjoying every second of it.

THE END

CUFFED
AT MIDNIGHT

Chapter One

The House-warming Gift

T REVOR SAT IN THE OFFICE on the third floor of their home working on a couple of cases George had forwarded to him. The days had flown by since their move to Ireland only a few months back. Their first Christmas had been spent in the new house in Dublin; although it had been filled with joy, it had also left him with a heavy heart. His parents' absence was never as painful as during holidays and special occasions. He had never spent those days—Christmas, New Year's, and birthdays— away from them, always making it a point to fly home.

He was home, now—for longer than he had ever been in the last dec- ade—and yet, they were not there. It was only a few days into the New Year, and in another week or so he would go through the same barrage of emotions again. His birthday was approaching, bringing with it the flood of memories of birthdays enjoyed with them. But maybe this year things would be different. This year he had a lot to be thankful for. Cassandra.

His wife, never one to sit still, was currently taking down the Christmas decorations from the tree in the family room. Music from the media center blasted through the rooms and he could hear her singing along, off-tune. Trevor was filled with an overwhelming sense of contentment and the beginning of a smile tipped the corners of his mouth. He was living the dream.

The Stars Wars-themed door chime cut through the pounding music. Startled, Trevor frowned and pushed away from his desk. He walked to the window, pushed the curtain aside, and looked at the street below. A small lorry was parked out front, a man jumping out of the cab. Trevor turned away and headed for the stairs, yelling down to Cassandra, "*A ghrá!?* Did you order anything for delivery!?"

"No! Why?" Her voice was full of curiosity as she met him at the stairs.

"Dunno. Didn't you hear the bell?" Cassandra shook her head and returned to singing Karaoke-style as she plucked decorations from the tree. He shrugged and continued his path down the next flight to the main floor. He opened the door to a man in a local delivery company uniform.

"Mr. and Mrs. Bauer?" the delivery man asked, looking up from his clipboard.

"Yes. I'm Mr. Bauer."

He thrust the clipboard at Trevor. "Sign here." He pointed to where Trevor needed to sign, turned on his heel, and headed back to the lorry, returning with a parcel.

"Where should I put it?"

"By the door is fine." Puzzled, he watched the delivery guy head back to the truck and return with another box, setting it beside the first.

The delivery man took the clipboard from Trevor's hands, scrutinized it, nodded, and walked away calling out, "Good day!"

"You too, mate," Trevor called, closing the door. He studied the boxes and noticed an envelope attached to one of them. He picked it off the box and removed a nice card from its folds.

Bottoms up! I know you guys will need to come up for air sometime. Until that happens, good thing I found this neat little store in Dublin that allowed me to save you from starvation.

A big smile spread across his face. He retrieved the boxes from the floor and carried them upstairs to the kitchen next to the family room where Cassandra was just about done with her dismantling of Christmas. Taking the boxes to the counter, he opened them and laughed out loud at what he found inside. He began to pull the items out and set them on the counter for Cassie's perusal: a case of Guinness, an assortment of frozen casseroles, and a box of scented bath oils.

"Who was at the door?" Curiosity colored Cassandra's voice.

"We had a special delivery. A very special delivery. Come see."

"Delivery? Did you order something?" Excitement flooded her expression. "A new tech toy? Let me see," she demanded, approaching the counter.

Trevor's grin grew wider as he handed her the card. Puzzled, she took it and read while he continued to unbox the items, placing them all on the counter. A moment later, her laughter resonated in the kitchen and wrapped around his heart like a velvet robe. "Belated house-warming gift? That is so Jessica."

Trevor smiled into Cassandra's eyes. "We should invite her for a visit and get her out on the town. We could take her to the Octagon Bar for a couple of pints. Maybe a stop at Lillies's Bordello after?"

Her eyes sparkled with humor. "A meet at The Octagon Bar sounds perfect. And Lillie's is a guaranteed good time. She'll have a blast. I'll bug her when she calls tomorrow."

Cassandra read the card again, still shaking her head, and examined the items lined up on the counter. She picked up the box of oils and waved it at him, wiggling her eyebrows. "Oh, man, she left no stone unturned."

"She sure didn't."

Cassandra removed the plastic wrapping from the box and slipped the oils out, setting them side by side. She brought the bottles to her nose, one by one, inhaling each scent. "Hmm."

A scarlet blush covered her cheeks when she realized he had been intently observing her actions with a wicked grin on his face. "What? Just trying to see what they smell like."

"And?"

"They smell really lovely and delicious." She looked at the assortment and called out their fragrances, "Sweet Almond, Lavender Sandalwood, Spicy Pear, Vanilla, and Keyano Chocolate."

His eye travelled the length her body. "I wonder how they'll smell on your skin." He looked into her eyes with feigned innocence. "You do know that scents change in contact with human skin depending on the person's body chemistry, right?"

Cassandra crossed her arms in front of her and returned his gaze with a condescending look on her face, full of hidden laughter. "And your point is?"

Trevor clicked his tongue. "I think we need to try them all. Make sure the scent works with yours."

Trevor's eyes strayed to the swell of her breasts accentuated by her crossed arms. His cock twitched and thickened, pushing against his jeans as he imagined trailing his nose along her skin, breathing her in. "I might need to cover your body with those and then smell each inch of you just to make sure. We don't want a scent incident."

He picked up the bottle of Keyano Chocolate and read the label. "Hmm. Edible. I think I just fell in love with Jessica's mind," he chuckled, wiggling his eyebrows wickedly at Cassandra.

"Hey! I don't share." She plucked the bottle from his fingers. "Edible, you say? I call dibs on the chocolate." Cassandra looked him dead in the eyes and licked her lips. "I will be licking that one off you." She shrugged innocently, "All in the spirit of preventing a 'scent incident.' Just saying." She grinned as she gathered up the oils. "Well, back to work. Still have a bit to do."

"Not so fast, Cassie girl." Trevor pinned her with his crisp blue gaze and stepped around the counter.

Cassandra laughed and bolted for the door. "I'll just put these away in the bathroom."

Trevor lunged after her, but she was faster. He watched as she scrambled up the stairs, laughing triumphantly. Halfway up she turned to look down at him and blew him a kiss. He narrowed his eyes playfully. "Payback, Cassie. Payback."

She moved out of sight in the direction of the bedroom calling out, "Yeah, yeah. Promises, promises."

Chapter Two

Stashed Treasure

CASSANDRA'S HEART FLUTTERED WITH PANIC. She caught her anxious expression in the bathroom mirror. Brows furrowed, eyes tight—all the signs of a freak-out. Only a few more days until Trevor's birthday and she was at her wits' end. What could you give to a geek who had everything? Their link to Brennan Enterprises gave them access to technological marvels still in development. On a personal level, their arsenal of tech gadgets was off the hook. Her desperation to find the perfect gift had built to such a high level that she had even contacted Stephan who, in turn, had been of no help at all. Her thoughts returned to the day of their conversation.

"Stephan! You have to help me."

"Cassandra," Stephan had laughed heartily. *"Slow down, lass. What is it? What's wrong?"*

"Trevor's birthday. That's what's wrong!"

Stephan's deep chuckle had flowed out of the handset. *"Is that all? Hold on. Did you say his birthday?"*

Cassandra had heard the rustling of pages. *"Shite. The fifteenth. Damn it; how could I have forgotten?"*

"What should I get him? Give me some ideas."

"Give you ideas? You? I wanted your help. You're supposed to tell me. Damn it." Exasperated, Cassandra had flopped on the couch and dropped her head back. She had tightened her grip on the handset.

"What do I do, Stephan? The damn man has everything. It needs to be special. It has to be. It's his first birthday we will spend together—" her voice had trailed off.

A heavy sigh had reached her across the line. *"I'm sorry lass. I don't know what to tell you. I have no idea what to get him, either. It's been a while since I have done anything more than call to wish him Happy Birthday."*

Cassandra had hissed through her teeth, disappointment coloring her voice. *"Geez Stephan. So much for being my go-to guy. I guess I'm back to square one."*

"Sorry I wasn't more helpful."

"Me too. But I'm taking solace in the fact that I'm not the only one stressing now."

"Yes. I would like to thank you for changing the whole tone of my day." There had been a trace of laughter in his voice.

Cassandra had pictured his sapphire blue eyes pinning her with sarcasm and had burst out laughing. *"Glad to be of assistance. Goodbye, Stephan."*

"Goodbye, lass."

That conversation had taken place a few days before, and Cassandra was still no closer to finding a fitting gift. "This is ridiculous. Seriously. Come on, Cassie. Think. It's just a damn gift," she muttered, turning on the tap and running her fingers under the stream. The cool water pooled in her cupped hands and she splashed her face with it, pressing her wet palms against her heated cheeks. "Think!"

She patted the towel bar. Finding it empty, she cursed and reached under the sink to grab one. Instead of finding a soft fluffy towel, her hand knocked over bottles. The sound of them toppling reminded her of the day she put them there. A wide smile spread across her face and a gleam filled her eyes.

A tingling of excitement raced through her as she dropped to a squat and sat back on her heels. Inside the cabinet were the oils that Jessica had given them. Cassandra's gentle laugh rippled through the air as she took hold of one of the bottles. Straightening, she leaned against the vanity. Her mind was racing a mile a second.

She laughed out loud, ran back into the bedroom, and pulled open the closet doors. In the corner of the large walk-in closet were two boxes. After rummaging through them for a little while, Cassandra breathed out a cry of relief and fist-pumped the air. She felt a rush of adrenaline course through her veins as she grabbed her treasure and stashed it under her side of the bed, out of plain sight. With a deep sense of satisfaction, she tidied up, leaving no traces of her wild pursuit. *He won't know what hit him.*

★ ★ ★ ★ ★

Cassandra had been behaving strangely for days. Trevor couldn't put his finger on the source of the devious smiles that peeked out time and again when she thought he wasn't watching. Something was up. He knew in his gut. Frowning, he tried to focus on the new assignment, but the transcripts were not anchoring his attention. He leaned back in his chair and gazed blindly at the wall, mind scurrying around the little tidbits he had picked up over the last two days.

She'd better not be planning a surprise birthday party for him. He didn't want anyone but her, preferably naked, with him on his birthday. As if summoned by his thoughts, Cassandra chose that minute to walk into the office. Again, she had that sneaky smile in her eyes, like she had a secret she had no intention of sharing with him.

"Have you talked to Stephan lately?"

"Nope. Why? Everything okay with him and Terese?" Cassandra sat at her desk across from his and maintained a steady expression during the exchange, but he could almost hear the trembling laughter in her voice.

"Nothing." Trevor studied her for a while until she raised her eyes to his.

"What?"

"You didn't plan a surprise party, did you? I told you I don't want it. I want to spend tomorrow with you, and only you."

"And I told you I have no plans for a party. Stephan has plans with Terese. Dad just signed a new client and has been personally overseeing the initial project setup. Even if I wanted to have Dad come for a quick visit, he couldn't. Jessica has no plans to come over anytime soon—she has a new beau. And George? He's worse than you are when it comes to being dragged away from his lair at Cryptocity. There you have it. I have nothing to hide." The sincerity of her words was subtly betrayed by the constant sparkle of humor in her eyes.

He considered the possible reasons she would be acting so strangely and a sudden thought popped into his mind. His stomach sank. "You're pregnant."

"Are you losing your mind?" Cassandra burst out laughing, clearly shocked and amused by his theory. "What have you been drinking?"

"I just know you're up to no good. You have that look you get when you dig up something juicy on a case."

Cassandra shook her head and rolled her eyes. *Oh yeah, she's up to something all right.* He could swear sometimes he heard the turbines turning in her head. But all he could do was sit back and watch as the wind picked up force.

Chapter Three

It's Midnight

CASSANDRA'S EYES CRACKED OPEN AT the first buzz of her phone. In the dim lighting provided by the full moon, she hurried to kill the alarm set to vibrate at midnight. It was Trevor's birthday, and she wanted to give him a memorable start to the day.

Anticipation coursed through her veins as she carefully rolled over and reached under the bed for the two service handcuffs she had stashed there a couple of days before. It was a shame she hadn't thought of the idea earlier or she could have ordered a nice lined pair, but these would do the trick just the same.

She gingerly scooted from the bed and stood next to it. Trevor's slow, drawn-out breaths had not changed rhythm. Confident he was still out cold, she let out the breath she had been holding in a quiet whoosh. *Perfect. Already on his back.* She wouldn't have to adjust her plan of attack.

Trevor's arm was stretched toward her side of the bed. A wicked grin curved her lips as she took his arm in her hands and shifted it in a smooth motion closer to the headboard post. She wrapped the first bracelet around his wrist and the other to the post. She carefully adjusted the ratchet so his hand couldn't slip through and eased a pillow closer to cradle it. Trevor stirred. Cassandra froze, her hands still on his wrist. Her heart pounded so hard she thought it would burst from her chest. She sighed in relief when he settled in his sleep. Her pulse beat wildly in her ears as she let go of his wrist and stepped back from the bed.

Her hands shook slightly and her knees were a little unsteady as she walked to the other side of the bed and repeated the process with the other wrist. The hardest part was over. Trevor's breath was still shallow and soft, he was none the wiser as to what had just happened to him. A deep sigh of relief escaped her. She stepped back and admired her handiwork. *So far so good. Really your fault, you know—issuing me a challenge.*

Cassandra padded to the foot of the bed. *Time for phase two.* She gripped the sheet in both hands and pulled it slowly it toward her. As it whispered down the length of Trevor's body, a wave of goose bumps spread across his skin and his nipples hardened in reaction to the change in temperature. The sight of his taut muscular body sent a flare of heat from her chest to her core.

Once she had control of the need burning through her, Cassandra pulled the sheet off the rest of the way and gently climbed onto the end of bed. She sat back on her knees and gazed at the feast before her.

Her eyes glided along the tight muscles of his arms to his chiseled cheekbones and firm lips. She was tempted to lick every inch of him. *Follow the plan, Cassie!* She had spent too much time planning this little adventure to see it ruined by her weakness for him.

She sat back and explored him with her loving gaze. The long eyelashes, five o'clock shadow, the relaxed boyish look on his face—so different from the intense probing one he normally wore when awake. She was still in awe of the events that had brought them together and at how hard they had fallen for each other in just a short time. *A lifetime for us.*

Cassandra's eyes moistened and a lump filled her throat, threatening to choke her. *Damn, she loved him.* She squeezed her eyes tight and took a deep silent breath, preparing for what lay ahead. She moistened her dry lips at the sight of his broad chest and the dusting of hair that traveled in a line down his tight abdomen to merge with the curl of hair that hugged the base of his cock. She leaned forward, pulling her hair back with her hand so it wouldn't tickle his skin, her pulse tapping a rapid rhythm in her ears and her breath shaky. A physical reaction to the daring move she was about to pull. After a moment's hesitation, she went for it, running the tip of her tongue along the inside of his knee. His muscles twitched at her moist touch and he unconsciously moved his leg away. Cassandra pulled back, expecting him to open his eyes. A wide grin spread across her face when they didn't.

More confident now, she picked up where she left off—trailing along his inner knee and across his thigh, enjoying the salty taste of his skin on her tongue. When she reached the juncture of his groin and thigh, she struck, sucking the soft skin into her mouth. Trevor jerked awake, struggling against the cuffs, which rattled against the bed. "What the fuck!"

A throaty laugh escaped her as she pinned his leg down and licked the little hickey she had left there. His struggles subsided and, for a second, she thought he had resigned himself to his situation, but as she raised her eyes, she found him sporting a narrowed, stormy glare. "What the hell do you think you're doing, Cassie girl?" he growled, pulling on the cuffs.

"Playing?" She grinned innocently at him.

"Playing with fire, more like it," Trevor grumbled, still not quite appreciating the idea of being rendered captive.

He squirmed with unease when she climbed up and straddled his thighs. Cassandra chuckled, thrilled by the tense expression on his face. He had the looks of someone who had never been in such a submissive position before.

Trevor held her gaze, hesitated a moment, taking her measure, then settled back against the pillows. The line had been crossed and he would definitely be using that against her at a later date. All kinds of thoughts regarding possible situations where those handcuffs could come in handy peppered his mind. "You know the saying, 'payback is a bitch'?"

"Yeah, you said it before." Cassandra flashed a sassy grin toward him.

He quirked an eyebrow. "Remember those words, Cassie girl. Remember them well."

A burst of laughter escaped her and she ran her nails along the inside of his thighs, smiling wider as his skin shivered and legs twitched. Her whiskey-brown eyes clung to his as she continued her slow stroking torture along his thighs.

"Would you like to know what time it is, *a ghrá?*"

He tried to decipher her question amidst the jumbled mess created in his head by her warm touch on his skin. She smiled softly at the confused look that must have colored his face.

"It's midnight. Happy Birthday!"

A lazy smile crept across his face. "You're handcuffing me to the bed as a birthday present?" She nodded and Trevor shook his head, a wider smile now flashing across his face. Only his wife would have thought of that little birthday surprise. "Are these our service cuffs?" A devious smile curved her lips as she nodded again, causing the tawny waves of her hair to frame her face. He chuckled softly. He could definitely say the handcuffs had now seen everything in the line of duty.

His breath stalled when she slid along his body until her face came even with his. She lowered her lips to his and breathed against them, "Happy birthday, my love." She ran her tongue seductively along the seam of his lips and slipped it between them, invading his mouth, circling, teasing his tongue into a sensual play, tasting every last inch of it.

He tried to take control of the kiss but she pulled away before he had a chance. "Cassie," he groaned.

"Just relax and enjoy your first birthday present of the day," she whispered.

He raised his eyebrows and jerked on the cuffs, grumbling, "How can I, like this?"

Cassandra sat back on his stomach, pulled off her silky tank top, and shook out her hair. "I'll help you," she grinned, tossing the top on the floor.

Trevor tugged at the cuffs, hard-pressed to find a way to touch her, but he couldn't even come close to it. "I am still not sure I can appreciate it this way. I need to touch you, kiss you."

"You don't need your hands to kiss me…and I will be doing the touching." Her wicked tone sent a jolt of electricity through his system and shorted his brain.

A groan rumbled in his chest and he shifted. "But you know how I like sinking my hands in your hair when I'm loving you. How I like to bury my fingers in you."

A low moan resonated deep in Cassandra's throat and she swallowed tightly. "How about you let me take the lead this time around? I promise you won't be disappointed. Besides, you really have no choice." She grinned mischievously, wiggling her eyebrows.

His eyes followed the graceful line of her neck, the pulse beating wildly at its base, and her beautiful breasts with their rosy puckered tips begging to be kissed. His hooded eyes met hers again and he flashed a wicked grin. "Come closer, then."

She bent over him, kissed his neck and his chest just above his heart. He closed his eyes tight in reaction to the touch of her lips on his skin, burning him, branding him. "Nope, not happening just yet." Her voice was a whisper, deep and sensual, sending a ripple of desire through his core. She slipped back down to the foot of the bed and he became lost in the moment, expecting her to take him in her mouth at any second, expecting to be hurled into a vortex of pleasure. Instead, he was brought to the present by the bump on the bed when she climbed off. His eyes snapped open. "Hey!" he yelled out. "What the hell! You're walking away? Where you going!?"

"You'll see!" she called back from the bathroom.

Cassandra opened the vanity cabinet and pulled out the bottle of Keyano Chocolate body oil she had called dibs on the day they had arrived. *He did say they were edible.* Giggling at the pun, she returned to the bedroom and placed it on the bed. She could feel the heat of Trevor's gaze as she pushed the thin fabric of the black lace thong off her hips and stepped out of it. Crawling back on the bed, she showed him the bottle.

"I called it."

He lifted his head and squinted at the label. Understanding seeped into him and he dropped his head back on the pillow. "Ah, hell!"

Cassandra smiled wickedly and poured a liberal amount of the oil on her hands. Trevor licked his lips, watching closely as she rubbed her hands together, spreading the oil evenly before gliding them across his chest. The heated sensation coupled with the slickness and sweet scent played havoc on her senses—and they must have affected Trevor too, because her name was a rasp on his lips, "Cassie."

Cassandra continued to spread and knead the slick oil into his skin and, unable to resist any longer, took one of his hard nipples in her mouth, sucking and grazing it with her teeth.

A satisfied hum sounded in her throat, "I know it's a woman thing, but you taste even better dipped in chocolate."

At her little tease, Trevor pulled at the cuffs again. A persuasive look covered his face and he urged in a low Irish drawl, "Set me free, Cassie girl. I want to touch you, *a ghrá.*"

Cassandra looked him straight in the eyes and licked the oil coating her lips, enjoying the smooth chocolaty taste of it. *Nice choice, Jessica.* "Not yet. I haven't finished giving you your gift. Besides, I told you I'd be the one doing the touching first."

His eyes tracked her every move. Cassandra knew she was playing with fire, just as he'd said. But it was a flame she couldn't resist. Like a moth attracted to light, she was more than willing to burn if it meant she would experience the flaming heat coursing through her to the fullest.

She poured a little more of the oil into her palms and smoothed it along the ridges of his abs and tight muscular thighs, now tighter since their workouts had begun. Her hands and fingers continued their journey, skimming along his groin and down to his calves, kneading tense muscles.

"Damn, I've missed something," Cassandra cursed and moved off the bed to the nightstand. She felt the laser heat of his stormy blue eyes boring into her as she turned on the iPod and their favorite song filled the room.

Holding eye contact with him, she stroked her fingers along his leg as she walked to the end of the bed. She stood at his feet and continued to pamper him, working the oil into the arch of his foot and along the top. She could feel the tension bleeding from him. He closed his eyes and relaxed his head back on the pillow.

"Damn, that feels good. I never knew you were so talented with your hands," he breathed out in a husky whisper.

Cassandra's soft laughter followed. "Consider it one of my hidden talents you were so interested in unveiling."

Trevor lifted his head slightly and cracked an eyelid before falling back to the pillow with a wide grin on his face.

Damn—that's not good! That grin always means trouble. Wondering at what he was thinking, she shifted to the other foot, giving it the same attention. From his feet, she worked her way up his calves, enjoying the view of his erection twitching with each touch of her fingers.

How can a foot massage be so fecking erotic? And yet it was. As Cassandra climbed back up on him, the beautiful view awed him. Miles of delicious skin waiting to be touched and massaged the same way she was touching, massaging him. *If only my hands were free.*

Settling back on his thighs, her fingers pressed into his skin and were everywhere—touching, stroking, massaging—driving him crazy. His cock pulsed with each contact and his need to have her intensified. He could feel the heat and dewy moisture between her legs where her sex pressed against his thigh. His thoughts narrowed to one. He wanted to drive into her, to feel her wet, hot sheath surrounding him, burning him. "Cassie. Please. Release me."

She brushed his pleas aside and continued with her little sensual play— massaging and touching forgotten regions of his body. Jolts of electricity sparked from his head to his toes under her assault. He strained against the cuffs with each touch. Exhausted from his forced restraint he raised his head to meet her eyes and implored, "Fecking hell! Don't make me wait any longer. *I need* to touch you."

As soon as the words fell from his lips, she pressed the length of her body against his, kissed his neck again, and locked eyes with him. Trailing her hand between them, she fisted his shaft, squeezing it gently, pumping it in a lazy up and down motion.

"Cassie! Now, damn it. Release me. Not like this. I need to be inside you," he growled harshly. He raised his torso from the bed, reaching for her, seeking her mouth with his.

When her lips touched, his heart pounded wildly. Trevor could have sworn the organ would burst from his chest. He leaned forward to take the kiss deeper, but she pulled back out of reach.

"Do you mean here?" she whispered, shifting her hips and rubbing his shaft against her wetness. Or maybe..." Without warning, she eased down his body to settle between his legs. Trevor raised himself as far as he could, his restraints cutting into his flesh as he struggled against them, and stared down at her. Her soft eyes held a glint of mischief as she took his cock in her hand and fisted its length. She rubbed the dewy crown across her lips mimicking a lipstick. "...Here?" The warm moist whisper of her words flowed over him before she took the whole of his shaft into her mouth, swallowing him to the hilt.

"Fuck!" he cried out as she rode his length with her mouth. The deep vibration of her chuckle rolled along the length of his cock and his hips surged again and again, pumping against her mouth. She took him in, feasting, swirling her tongue around the underside of his engorged head and its sensitive nerve endings. He threw his head back on the pillow, his body bowed with the tension, and he released a guttural moan of pleasure as a primal heat of desire coursed him at the pulls of her mouth.

"Gods, Cassie! So. Fucking. Good." She took him deeper still and eased back slowly until the silky hood of his cock was at her lips. The scraping of her teeth on his highly sensitive crown sent an arrow of pleasurable pain through his entire body, blurring his vision.

"Cassandra!" His cry echoed in the room as he plunged into her mouth, his hips bucking in tandem with the pulsing of his cock. A low moan revved in Cassandra's throat, sending a shiver up Trevor's spine. Her pace increased, pumping along his length. Her soft tongue danced and twisted around him, licking him from tip to base, driving him to sheer insanity. Swirling and flicking around his crown, she continued to suck and swallow him.

"Fuck, Cassie!" he exploded, struggling with the cuffs. "Cassie girl, release me now!" he commanded, shifting his hips away from her. She pulled him from her mouth and, released from the pressure, he fell back to the bed. His lungs sawed and he tried to suck in air.

Relieved, he closed his eyes tight, expecting her to open the cuffs and allow him to touch her at last—hold her, roll her on the bed, and mount her as he craved. His cock was on the verge of erupting and his balls were tight and heavy. He knew he was very close to reaching a blessed and much-needed release, but he wanted more of her. When nothing happened, his eyes popped open, heart racing and pounding in his ears. The woman had a dominatrix streak to her. That was the only possible explanation to her little birthday surprise. Her body, a distraction to his senses, the bait to get him under her control, it seemed. He would have to sleep with one eye open from now on. Or hide the damn cuffs for his own use later.

"Cassie? Now!" *Yes, payback is coming.* Trevor thought to himself, considering all options he had for providing her with the same sensual torture and sexual tension he was experiencing at that moment. He took a deep breath and her scent erased every single logical thought in his mind. "Come on, babe. Let me go."

Cassandra grinned at his frantic demand. She had no intention of releasing his wrists just yet. She wasn't finished with him. She smiled into his desperate face, held his fevered gaze as she lowered herself to continue what she had started. Cassandra took him in her hand again and proceeded to lick and nip along the underside of his shaft. The sweet intoxicating musk of his body almost overwhelmed her and her breasts tingled against the satin fabric of the sheet. She caressed his sac gently, rolling his balls in her hand and pushing him farther. He strained against the cuffs, hips bucking against her hand.

"Inside you, love. Ride me, Cassie," he begged trying to pull away.

Cassandra flashed a wicked grin at him and felt powerful in the knowledge that she could bring him to the boiling point so fast, so easy. She sat on her heels to look at her husband, her man. Her eyes reveled at the strength of his flesh. He lay deceivingly helpless on his back, his skin covered in a thin layer of sweat, a direct result of her ministrations. A hot ache grew in her throat. She wanted him to remember that night for a long, long time. Tempting him even more, she slid her body against his, skimming her breasts along his chest until they were face to face. Her heart skipped a beat or two at the pulse of his erection pressed against her stomach between them. She captured his gaze, his eyes darkened to the deepest indigo blue, and held it while she adjusted herself until the tip of his cock pressed against the wet folds of her sex. A delicious shiver of need ran through her.

"You're killing me, *a ghrá*," he rasped harshly, closing his eyes and gasping for breath.

In one single strike, Cassandra descended upon him and impaled herself to the hilt. A long drawn-out moan escaped her. "Sh-i-i-te!" he uttered, pressing his head back into the pillow and thrusting his hips against hers, driving himself deeper.

Having her wet sheath around him, enveloping him, felt like balm to his soul. His breath hitched in his lungs with the intensity of the moment. Without thinking, Trevor reached out to hold her hips, touch her skin, only to feel the grip of the cuffs cutting into his wrists. "Damn it to hell!"

"Just feel it, Trev. Feel me, taking you deep." Her words were like kindle to the fire already flaming high inside him. Trevor leveraged his weight on his feet and thrust his hips, grinding against her core, feeling the moisture of her juices coat the juncture of their bodies as they moved against each other.

Heat rolled off Cassandra in waves. She moaned and ground down hard against him, leveraging on her knees and meeting him thrust for thrust. She leaned toward him and caught his mouth in a deep searing kiss. Her tongue invaded his mouth, thrusting, demanding, imitating the tempo of his own thrusts. Almost lost to the burn of her lips, Trevor was startled by the rustling of her hand under his pillow, patting, reaching for something. *Please let it be the fucking key.*

Once she found what she was looking for, she cupped his face murmuring against his lips, "Oh man I am gonna burn for this. I know I am." She deepened the kiss, drawing a tattered moan from him as they sucked and bit each other's lips in total abandon.

"God, Cassie. I want to touch you bad...hold your hips tight, dig my fingers in your soft skin as I drive into you." Trevor's words broke through his lips in jagged breaths. He groaned as she continued to assault his mouth in the same cadence as she was taking his cock.

His mind swirled with the pleasure of the experience. She had given him everything without taking anything in return. It finally hit him. He didn't need to be in charge. He trusted her with all of himself. She owned him true—mind, body, and soul. Perfectly suited that on this day, his birthday, he found the full acceptance of the fact he belonged to her when once he had felt so lost and adrift—a rebirth in her arms. "Cassie girl."

His cock pulsed when the first fingers of her climax squeezed him. With a gasp, she released his mouth and arched her back, exposing her taut nipples to his eyes while reaching in between them with her fingers. His gaze was riveted on her, her hands, and to the sensuality of the act. She rubbed her glistening folds, circling and massaging the bud of her sex, bringing her closer to her release. "I'm so close, love." She ground harder against him as his thrust became frantic. "Trevor. More." She lifted and ground harder down against him as his thrust become frantic.

"Yes, baby. Come for me. Yes!" His body trembled as he reached the end of his control. "With me, Cassie girl. Come with me. I want to feel you."

Her inner walls quivered around his shaft in an intimate massage. His balls tightened and the twinge of his release spilled down his spine. "Yes!"

Trevor's release broke at the same time her insides exploded in contractions, squeezing him tight in the wake of her wild ride. Once the high of the wave had passed, she collapsed on his chest in a boneless heap. Heart hammered against his, she tucked her head in the crook of his neck. Her hair spread wildly over his shoulder, her breasts erect and hard, pressing against his chest. She ground her sex against his, pushing his still-erect cock further in as a throaty moaned escaped her parted lips.

"I could take you all over again," she whispered hoarsely.

Trevor chuckled and rubbed his face against her head. "Promise me?"

A small giggle filled his ear. "I thought you'd be mad now."

"God. This was the second most fulfilling experience of my life."

"Second?" She lifted her head and stared at him with questioning eyes.

"Yes. Second to the first time I took you. That was when I knew I was yours. You can take me any way you want, *a ghrá*." The laughter faded from his eyes as he quietly asked, "I need to hold you now babe. Release me."

"Oh, shit." She laughed and searched around them until she picked something from the mussed folds of the bed sheets. "Got it!" She pulled out the little key and unlocked his left wrist. The skin around his wrist was red and raw from his struggles against the restraints. "Trev!" She pulled his wrist to her lips and kissed it gently. "I never thought...damn."

Free to touch her, he dug his fingers into her hair, palmed the back of her head, and brought her lips to his. He kissed her softly, sensing her concern. "Don't fret, Cassie, it was so worth it. Now, love, the other." Her heart fluttered wildly in her chest as she kissed him back, leaned over to repeat the process, and freed him.

Finally able to reach out and touch her as he wanted, Trevor gathered her in his arms, held on to her tight, breathed her in just to feel her seeping underneath his skin. "Thank you for the memorable birthday. It will never be forgotten." He rested his chin on her head, sighing in content and fulfilled happiness. "My first birthday with you. My first birthday feeling whole again. You are half of me, my love." He dropped a kiss on her head as Cassandra tucked her thigh between his. Their bodies entwined, she slipped into a restful sleep while Trevor grinned and planned his payback.

THE END

PASSION AT DAWN

"We're never so vulnerable than when we trust someone—but paradoxically, if we cannot trust, neither can we find love or joy."
—Walter Anderson

Chapter One

Let's Talk About Sex

THE SUN SHONE BRIGHTLY THROUGH the big glass windows facing St. Stephen's Green, casting a warm glow across the wooden floors as Trevor jogged down the stairs to the family room. He'd soaked in the shower longer than he'd planned, letting the hot water ease the tension from his muscles—a tension created by frustration over the lack of chatter tied to his quest, as well as some tough NSA cases hitting Operation Countermeasure.

Stepping off the stairs, he found Cassandra curled up on the comfy sofa engrossed in what appeared to be a fashion magazine. Trevor grabbed an energy drink from the fridge and flopped beside her. Cassandra barely registered his presence; curious at her focus on the read, he glanced at the open pages. A chuckle spontaneously bubbled in his chest and he raised an eyebrow.

"Cosmo?"

"What? What's wrong with *Cosmopolitan?"* Her eyes remained locked on the pages, enthralled by whatever she was reading.

Trevor scoffed. "All of that stuff in there is nonsense. They have no clue what a guy thinks. What gives them the idea they know the 'truth'?" He illustrated the quotation marks with his fingers as he shook his head. His wife, the most sensible woman he knew, reading up on relationship tips. Go figure.

Her eyebrows elevated in conjunction with her tone. "Hold on a second. It isn't always about what a man thinks." She flashed the article she was reading: "A Month of Hot Sex Ideas." "What you're telling me is that all the tips on how to warm up a marriage, how to please a man, and everything else in here is all bullshit? All of it?"

Trevor shrugged. "And why would anyone need that anyway?" He frowned. *What am I missing?* "I thought we did pretty well in that area, no?"

Cassandra laughed, unaware of the onslaught of worry peppering his mind. "We do pretty well, but you never know—I might come across new things we might want to try."

His eyebrows arched and he cocked his head, disbelief coloring his playful tone. "So, you're seriously telling me you're looking for stuff to try? In bed?"

"Well, not actively looking." Cassandra's mischief reared in her tone as she flipped the page. "But if I come across something intriguing...."

Trevor inhaled deeply. His pulse raced as sensual scenes crossed his mind—the contrast of their bare skins against each other, her moist, cool lips soothing his heated flesh. His thoughts bounced around, knocking his senses into high gear. He probed deeper, unable to hold back his curiosity about how far she'd take that tease. "What if you found something that piqued your interest?" He retrieved one of his tech gadget magazines from the coffee table and blindly paged through it, his attention covertly locked on her. "Something that you've never tried with anyone before.

Something totally outside your comfort zone. Would you still want to try it?" He kept his tone speculative, surreptitiously hiding the full extent of his interest in the subject.

From the corner of his eye, he saw Cassandra's head snap in his direction. He turned to face her and met eyes filled with a mix of interest and fire. His stomach tightened. He'd definitely captured her attention with that one little question.

"With you...anything."

Her response, emphasized by the spark in her eyes, sent him into overdrive as, once again, images of his wife—the softness of her skin under his, the curve of her breast in his hand—lit up his mind's eye.

He shook the tempting thoughts from his head. He wanted, needed to know where they stood in the exploration of their intimacy. His recklessness got the best of him. "What if I'm the one who has some crazy fantasy I've never experienced before with anyone?" He paused, uncertain of the answer he'd receive. "Would you be game?"

"So you do have fantasies aside from what we've done." An expression of humorous surprise blanketed her face.

If you only knew, love. "I don't think we've even scratched the surface of all we can do, a bhean." He grinned devilishly. "And you're avoiding the question. Would you?"

She smiled as she trailed her finger across his jaw and chin in a slow, tempting movement. Trevor's mouth went dry when she then rubbed her thumb back and forth across his bottom lip. "The answer remains the same." Her warm brown eyes held his gaze. "With you, anything."

He drew a sharp breath and a cheeky smile spread across his lips. "Glad to know you trust me that way."

"Likewise." She pressed her lips against his in a quick kiss and returned to reading as if the conversation had been completely inconsequential.

Trevor pulled her back against his chest and kissed the top of her head. While Cassandra continued to browse her magazine, he settled to watch

TV. He needed something to mute the loud chatter ringing in his ears. Always on the prowl for the latest gadgets, he tuned in to his favorite program on Channel 5, *The Gadget Show*. Finding a new geek toy would be the perfect solution for taking his mind off the mass of convoluted thoughts overwhelming him.

He rewound the show for the umpteenth time, his concentration shot. Their exchange kept banging in his head like a wrecking ball. Was it a sign that she wanted more from their relationship? Or a sign that she was pondering what else they could offer each other? A frown creased his brow. He couldn't tell by their short conversation. His eyes darted toward her when another chuckle spilled from her lips and she carefully dog-eared the page. It fueled his curiosity. "So, what's making you laugh? Have you found anything worth exploring?"

"Not really. Day twenty cracked me up. A striptease. Reminded me of us, actually."

A thick silence descended over the room while Trevor digested her comment. He was afraid to even ask why a striptease would remind her of them. Then visions of the straps of her lacy bra sliding down her arms and her pathetic excuse for panties grazing past her hips sent a rush of blood straight to his cock. He drew in a shallow breath and tiptoed around the subject again. "We never really talk much about that, do we?"

"About what? Sex? No." A saucy grin quirked the corner of her mouth as she flipped the page. "We just do it."

Trevor laughed at her unexpected witty retort. "We do, don't we? I think it's perfectly normal to want to jump the bones of the one you love, don't you?"

"I'd have to agree with you on that one. I love it when you jump my bones."

He turned in his seat to face her, all humor bled from his expression. "You'd tell me if you weren't getting what you wanted from me—from us, right?"

Cassandra framed his face with her hands, ran her tongue along his lips, then kissed him. "You worry too much, Trev. Six months is not enough time to learn everything there is to learn about each other."

"Hell. Sixty years won't be enough to sate the hunger I have for you, Cassie."

"I'm counting on that. Hmm, I have an idea." A mischievous sparkle shone in her eyes. "Maybe I should start a blog. Chart our course as we get to know each other over the next months, years, decades. I'm sure there are some tricks my geek can teach a few others out there." A devious smile quirked her lips. "Maybe submit it to Cosmo as a monthly column: 'My Sex Life with a Geek and His Hardware.' Hell, you have moves that—"

"What the fuck?! Don't you dare!" he burst out, laughing. "Shite! George would never let me live that one down. I can hear it now: 'Dude! You are so fucked when the guys see this.'"

Cassandra slid out of his arms, jumped up, and grinned down at him. "I think I'll start now."

A surge of adrenaline pumped in his veins. Trevor scrambled to his feet and gave chase. "Cassandra Cristina! You go anywhere near that computer and I'll have to spank you."

Her laugher echoed through the room as she took the stairs two at a time. "Like I've never heard that before."

Trevor cursed under his breath and caught her at the top of the stairs. Sweeping her up and over his shoulder, he slapped her ass.

"Hey! That stung. Trevor, put me down!"

"I will. No worries about that." In long strides, he headed toward their bedroom with his wiggling wife in his arms. In the back of his mind, he made a note to check out the article she had marked and see for himself what had perked her interest. Maybe get an idea or two from the magazine. In business and in love, it never hurt to diversify—and he was all for entrepreneurship.

Chapter Two

Delusional Bastard

TREVOR CLIMBED THE STAIRS TO the first-floor living space and set the grocery bags on the kitchen counter. He'd been gone almost an hour. Too much work and no play made for a very restless Trevor. He had needed to get out, breathe in crisp fresh air, and clear his head of the jumble it'd been. He and George had been pulled in on some great cases, most resolved with their ingenious infiltration skills. If only his own case could be solved that easily.

He pushed his sunglasses up on his head and unloaded his bounty from the bags. All the fixings to show off his cooking skills honed as a bachelor. Both he and Cassandra had been living off takeout the last few days and he wanted to make her a nice dinner. He would enjoy seeing the surprise on her face when he called her down to eat.

Putting the last of the items away, he tossed his sunglasses on the counter, grabbed a beer, and moved across the space to the couch. The late afternoon sun was a welcome relief from the heavy rain they had experienced for the past few days. The smells of spring—wet earth heating under the sun's rays, the smell of flowers beginning to bloom—wafted through the front windows, which were now cracked open for the first time since the thermometer had taken a nosedive in the fall.

From where he sat, he could hear the husky murmur of his wife's voice drifting down the stairs. *Probably deep in conversation with Jessie again.* Cassandra missed working side by side and hanging out with her best friend. She compensated for it with frequent calls overseas. *Thank God for the internet and chat applications.* Trevor shook his head and smiled as he flipped on the telly to check the latest football scores. He had a running bet with Stephan that the Sligo Rovers would take it all that season and he wanted to follow the matches closely.

"Bloody hell!" Trevor yelled a little while later when the ball missed the target again. The cheers of the fans blaring through the speakers almost muffled Cassandra's raised voice as it punched down the stairs. Curious, and a little concerned, he ran up to check on her. Irritation and defiance crowded her tone as he approached the office door and he wondered why her panties were in a bunch.

"Stop being an ass over this, Nate."

A fist tightened around his heart and a familiar angst simmered low in the pit of his stomach. The cause of her aggravation became crystal clear: Nelson.

After a brief pause, Cassandra snapped, "No. It's definitive. Get over it."

A heavy feeling he'd gotten to know well twirled in his chest. To his chagrin, the grudgingness flooding him was something he couldn't quite help or avoid when it involved the person on the other end of the line. He leaned against the doorjamb and folded his arms across his chest, listening, eyes locked on Cassandra's stiff posture, the tapping of her foot. From where he stood, he could see her frown deepen. The grip around his heart squeezed tighter.

She grew silent and then let out an exasperated sigh. "I gotta go. Have work to do. I'll be in touch when I have something for you." Cassandra's breath heaved out of her as she tossed her cell on the desk and leaned back in her chair. She brushed her hair from her face in frustration, a gesture Trevor knew well.

"Nelson giving you a hard time again?"

A startled yelp slipped from her lips. Cassandra swung her chair to face him. "Shit, Trevor! You shouldn't sneak up on me like that. How long have you been standing there?"

"Long enough." Trevor ground his teeth. He wasn't quite sure how to handle his feelings about the CIA operative. Nelson was one of those people that could get under one's skin in a bad way, and he had certainly crawled under Trevor's the few times he'd found an excuse to be in touch with Cassandra since their move to Dublin.

Trevor struggled to ignore the anger coiling in his stomach. He pushed away from the door. "I don't know whether to kick the crap out of him or just pity him." Cassandra tracked his progress toward his desk. He took his seat and huffed, "Nelson can go f—"

"—ind someone else to bother?" she finished his sentence with a quirked eyebrow, her gaze chastising. "He's a bit over the top sometimes and can be a royal pain in the ass. I'll give you that."

Trevor narrowed his eyes. Her eagerness to defend Nelson's behavior annoyed the hell out of him, but he knew she did it out of a warped sense of loyalty toward the man.

"Some of the comments and innuendos he's left hanging in the air are more than over the top. He's damn lucky I haven't flown to Langley to break his jaw," Trevor growled as he scrubbed his hair with his hands, turning it into more of a disheveled mess. Exhaling a deep breath, he linked his hands behind his head, and stared across the desks into her eyes. "It's clear he still holds a torch for you. Hell. He makes it crystal every chance he gets."

She scoffed. "He does not."

"Oh yeah, he does. That time he met us at the airport. The few times he's called here to talk about things that could easily have been handled over an email." His tongue was heavy with irritation. "Why can't he accept the fact that you've made your choice?"

Cassandra's gaze dimmed. "Nathan can be difficult, especially when his back's against a wall. I still blame myself for it. I honestly don't think he's gotten over the fact that I couldn't think of him as more than a friend."

"He's an adult, Cassie. Not a child. Love can flourish in the harshest environments, but only if the seed is there to begin with." Trevor's somber tone was a harsh contrast to his usual carefree one.

"I'm pretty sure he will eventually get it. Nathan is really a good guy at heart. He just needs someone to sweep him off his feet. Slap him upside his head."

"When he does find the saint that will put up with him, I hope he kicks him in the balls, too."

"Trevor!" She shook her head, but the disapproving glare in her eyes wavered under the humor bleeding through her voice.

"Hey, you never know," he shrugged.

Cassandra uncurled herself from her chair, closed the distance between them, and, straddling his hips, eased down onto his lap. She cupped his cheeks and looked deep into his eyes. "Let's not talk about him." She popped a kiss on his lips and then another. "There's nobody else in the world for me but you. Never has been."

Trevor sighed and ran his palms up and down her thighs, settling them on the small of her back. His pulse kicked into a hard beating drum, blood flowed hot through his veins. "I know. I have no doubt about that. But it doesn't change the fact he.... Never mind. He just rubs me the wrong way." His body warmed up considerably in those last few seconds, anger subsiding under her touch. "The alpha geek in me wants to brand you as mine in all possible ways, make it clear to Nelson and any other *eejit* that you are not available. You are *mine.*" He hated how he sounded—all "me Tarzan, you Jane"—but there was no other way to explain it.

"Trevor. Anyone in their right mind would see that I only have eyes for you."

He trained his gaze on her. "Anybody with the exception of Nelson. Delusional bastard." Trevor frowned, irritation burrowing under his skin once again.

Dropping another kiss on his lips, she eased off his lap. "Who knows, maybe one day the two of you will have a pint and laugh about it."

"Don't count on it," Trevor mumbled under his breath as he rose to his feet.

"What did you say?" Cassandra turned to look back at him, expectation in her questioning glance.

"Nothing." His mood had soured considerably from the time he'd walked in the house with plans to sweep her off her feet with a tempting meal.

"Wait." A wicked half grin curved the corner of Cassandra's mouth and desire flared in her eyes. "Did you say 'brand'? Hmm, time to pull out the magazine. I think I saw something that fits the bill."

A tingle ran through his body at her insinuation and a rush of blood pounded in his ears. His jaw twitched involuntarily and a smile tugged at his mouth as his irritation melted away for good. *How the hell does she do that? Disarm me and take the wind from my sails with one single strike?* On a long breath, he grabbed her by the hand and tugged her to the door. "Come on. Give me a hand with dinner."

"Oh! I get to play Sous-Chef. Okay, give me a sec to change into my sexy apron. I'll have to be careful to avoid splatters." Her expression took on a serious quality. "The apron doesn't cover much...."

Trevor stood, slack-jawed, and stared at her for a moment before he registered her teasing tone. Cassandra rolled her eyes and flicked his chin playfully. "Men. You really think I would cook naked?" She snorted. "Hell, no. I'm not putting—" she pointed to her round, full breasts, "—the girls in danger." She brushed past him. "Besides, you'd miss them too much if they became the casualty of a kitchen incident."

Trevor ran a hand over his face and watched as she skipped down the stairs, mesmerized by the sway of her ass encased in faded blue jeans, slung low on her hips, and the curve of her back peeking from the hem of her tight t-shirt. A vision of pushing her against the kitchen counter's smooth marble, licking, nipping her full lower lip while reveling in her softness, her heat, assaulted him. His body reacted instantly and he pressed his hand against the bulge in his pants to ease the ache.

"Move it, mister. I'm hungry," she called over her shoulder.

"Sweet Mary, she'll be the death of me," he mumbled in a ragged breath as he followed her down.

Chapter Three

Nice Surfaces

CASSANDRA MOANED AS SHE SAVORED the last bite of Trevor's culinary delights. The steak had melted in her mouth like butter, and everything else had been close to perfect. The only dark cloud on the horizon had been Trevor's brooding silence. From across the table she had watched him grow quiet through dinner.

He pushed the food on his plate around with his fork, his brow creased, his eyes lost in nothingness. Something was bothering him—and it was more than just Nathan's call.

She bridged the silence. "Did you and George come across anything new today?"

"Nothing. We were busy with the high-profile cases." His pensive expression told her he was lost in his own world.

"The CIA's?"

He tipped his eyes up and locked them on hers. "Yes. They sent us a new one, too. Actually, I need your take on it. It'll be interesting to get your thoughts on it from a psychological perspective." She loved seeing a renewed spark in him when he talked about intriguing cases.

"Sure. You know I'm always willing to lend a hand." She smiled widely at the prospect.

"This one's tough. The target they're looking for is technically unknown."

"What do you mean?"

Trevor set his fork down, at last giving her his attention. "Faceless. Nobody knows what he looks like. He's virtually a ghost. George and I are searching for a digital footprint we can trace."

"Hmm. That is interesting. If you have the case files, I'd like to take a look at them.

"You can have at it anytime. They're on the secure drive."

"Anything specific I should be looking for?" She reached for her wine.

"No. Just do your usual magic. I'm sure you'll find things we've missed."

"Will do." Cassandra lifted the glass to her lips and took a long swallow of the Cabernet Sauvignon. Even the delicious undertones of black cherry and dark chocolate couldn't distract her from her scrutiny. She waited for him to continue, share his concerns, but it never came.

A weird tightening sensation was starting to happen in her chest. Anxious for him to let go of what he was holding inside, she took a forward approach. "What else is wrong? You took off for a walk earlier. That always means something is eating at you." She set her glass down and leaned forward resting her elbows on the table. "Spill."

Trevor wiped his mouth, methodically folded his napkin, and set it in front of him. He ran his hand over his hair and, with a heavy sigh, sat back in his chair. "It's getting to me, Cassie. The not knowing."

Her heart skipped a beat at the vulnerability she saw in his stormy blue eyes. "It'll happen, you know," she tried to reassure him. "I feel it in my gut. Jessie and I check out new leads every day."

"We haven't had hits." He blew out a deep breath and rubbed both hands over his face. "This month has been dry. No solid leads. Even George is starting to twitch."

"It'll happen. You just have to believe. You're amazing at so many things." The knowledge of the origin of his worries fueled her need to jolt him out of his funk. She looked across the table with a smile in her eyes and lifted her glass in a toast. "Case in point: you, my gorgeous geek, are an excellent cook. It was very tasty. Just saying." She tilted her head to the side and glanced him over. "Any other hidden talents?" When a small smile lifted the corner of his mouth, she knew she'd succeeded.

Trevor tipped his chair back and lowered his voice, the Irish lilt accentuated in the rasped words. "Many, lass. You'd be surprised." Humor ran across his features and he shot her a lopsided grin, the one that always warmed her up a notch. His wickedness was back in full force. "You should try and dig a little more for them." Her cheeks warmed and he sat back with a satisfied, smug grin. Narrowing his eyes, he continued the tease. "How about you? Any hidden talents you feel compelled to share?"

Cassandra snorted. "If I told you, I'd have to kill you." She stood and gathered her dishes.

Trevor followed her to the counter with his. Mischief glinted in the depth of his eyes. "Maybe we could trade secrets. I tell you mine, you tell me yours. Fair trade."

"I'm sure that, with your skills, you'll find ways to infiltrate and uncover mine all on your own." She leaned against the marble counter and trailed her eyes from his chest to his groin. She let her eyes linger there a moment before returning them to his. She flashed him a naughty grin. "You have a mighty powerful tool in your arsenal."

Trevor roared in laughter and her grin dissolved into laughter of her own. Their gaze connected and their amusement slowly faded into awareness of a hunger not sated by the delicious meal. He held her gaze and closed the distance between them, caging her against the counter. His warm breath feathered her cheek when he lowered his face to hers. A knot formed in her stomach. She licked her lips and swallowed around the lump that pushed up her throat as his lips brushed the shell of her ear and a tingling spread along every inch of her skin. "Does Cosmo have a whole article on tools and their uses, Cassie girl?"

She held her breath, her body taut with arousal. "Ah...I mean...I need to...."

Trevor chuckled and looked at her in feigned astonishment as he continued to press his body against the length of hers. "What? No smart-mouth remark? No witty retort?"

Sparks of electricity fired across Cassandra's brain. All thoughts centered on Trevor, on the wicked things he could do to her, with her. His heady aftershave evoked images of sinful kisses on the beach wrapped in the warmth of his arms. She gazed back at him wordlessly.

"Geek got your tongue, *a ghrá*?" His eyes dropped to her lips and his crisp blue irises filled with torrid desire.

Cassandra's stomach bottomed out when he fisted the back of her hair and covered her mouth with his in a bone-melting, lip-crushing kiss. A whimper of pleasure rose inside her and a shaft of pure need shot straight to her clit. God, the man could kiss. His lips slanted across hers, nipping and sucking along her lower lip. She grabbed his shoulders to keep from collapsing like a puddle of want at his feet.

She hissed as his fingers skimmed along her ribs and he reached between them for the hem of her shirt. The contrast of the cool air in the house and the heat emanating from his hand sent shivers across her skin. His searing hot palm slid from her belly to the underside of her breast and cupped it. "Cassie," he groaned, plunging his tongue deep in her mouth. Her nickname spoken in his Irish singsong lilt always brought out the want in her. She moaned and reached for the waistband of his pants. She fumbled with the buttons of his jeans and dipped her hand inside. Her fingers wrapped around his thick, hard erection as their tongues continued their sensuous dance.

"Fuck!" Trevor pulled back from the kiss and jerked her t-shirt over her head, forcing her to release him in the process. She bunched his shirt up, seeking the touch of his skin on hers. With another curse, Trevor yanked his own shirt over his head and pulled her back to him. Their sighs mingled at finally reaching their goal. Cassandra's sensitive nipples scraped against his solid chest, sending a quiver of anticipation down her spine. Trevor nuzzled the tender skin of her neck, scraping his teeth along the curve where it met her shoulder.

Her breath quickened. "Jeezus, Trevor." Cassandra peppered kisses on his chest while she pushed his jeans off his hips with unsteady hands. "Do you ever think we could, just once, make it upstairs?"

He kicked his jeans to the side. "Why—" he exhaled in a harsh breath swiping his tongue across her jaw "—would we want to do that, when we have all these nice surfaces?" He grabbed her by the waist and swung her around, dumping her ass on the table.

"Trevor!" she cried out as the sounds of dishes clanking and crashing against each other—the remains of the dinner he'd shoved out of their way—echoed like musical notes around them.

"Don't worry. I'll handle the cleanup."

She smiled sweetly. "Another hidden talent?"

His sexy crooked grin pulled at her heart as his nimble fingers unzipped and tugged at her jeans, prompting her to help him get them off her hips. "Fuck, Cassie. Are these painted on?" His hot breath brushed her thighs as he bent over to wrench them from her legs. "Yes!" he chuckled, grinning widely as he displayed his prize—her panties and skin-tight jeans—dangling from a hooked finger. She laughed out loud and reached for him. Trevor tossed her jeans on the floor and stepped between her thighs.

"Hmm, is this dessert?" she breathed out as she skimmed her palms from his ribs to his shoulders and back to his waist.

His eyes flashed hot and Cassandra's tummy clenched when he brushed his thumbs across the soft skin on the inside of her knees. Her throat tightened as he slid her closer still and pressed his hard erection against the valley between her thighs.

"Dessert," his warm breath caressed her cheek. "Now, *that* is a brilliant idea." He pressed a hard kiss on her lips and tweaked her nipple. "Don't move."

"Hey! Where are you going?" She made a grab for him as he stepped away.

Trevor evaded her grasp and shot her a wicked grin over his shoulder while he walked to the refrigerator. "Don't move. I mean it."

He grabbed something from the fridge and stalked back to her. Cassandra's eyes flicked from the can of whipped cream back to his fiendish gaze and, in that moment, she knew exactly what he had in mind.

"I get dessert first. My reward for cooking. I'm sure you don't mind."

She sucked in a sharp gasp when Trevor kneeled and brushed the cold smooth surface of the can along the inside of her thigh to the juncture of her legs. The cold touch to her heated skin acted like a jolt of electricity. Her heart jumped straight to her throat. A hoarse moan fell from her lips and she leaned back to rest on her elbows when he followed the same path with his moist hot breath and tongue.

Cassandra saw her desire reflected in Trevor's eyes. The gleam of promise in his meant she would enjoy "dessert" as much as he would. Her mouth grew dry. She flicked her tongue across her lips in anticipation as Trevor shook the can and depressed the tip, deploying a stream of cream over her clit. He held her gaze as he set the can aside with slow, measured movements. He eased her thighs further apart and lowered his head to her expectant heat.

Her body collapsed against the table at the first touch of his mouth over her cream-covered bud. He capped her soft flesh in an open-mouthed kiss and sucked the sweet cream from her folds. "Trevor!" Her fingers dug in his hair, holding him to her, afraid he would stop if she let go, afraid she would die if she didn't.

A shiver raked up her back and her heart bucked against her ribs with each suck, lap, twirl of his tongue. A hiss of air and a second brush of cold contact jolted her again. Her head snapped up and she gazed down the length of her body to see another mound of cold cream blanketing her hot sex. Trevor licked her in a long, slow swipe of his tongue. Her body jerked and a burst of goose bumps peppered across her skin, pebbling her nipples to tight little peaks.

Cassandra slid her hand to her own breast and kneaded it, magnifying the pleasure of Trevor's teasing, flicking, sucking. A low hum vibrated in the air as he lapped the whipped cream and her own juices from her folds. Trevor's hand glided up her body, covered hers, and pulled it aside. He cupped her turgid breast and rolled her nipple between his forefinger and thumb while he nipped and sucked hard on her clit. "God, yes," she whispered in a slow exhale of breath, lifting, arching her back, undulating her hips against his lips and seeking his tongue.

Her taste overpowered his senses, her moans and the rocking of her hips against his lips guided him to take his fill of the decadent dessert, but his flesh wanted to meld with hers. A hot rush of blood pumped through him. His balls ached and his cock pulsed with life, begging to dive into her wet heat. He pushed to his feet, cupped the back of her neck, and brought her mouth to his, dipping his tongue between soft full lips. Cassandra instinctively dug her fingers in his ass, dragging him closer, voiding the distance between them.

In one stroke, he thrust deep, drawing ragged groans from them both. Need consumed him. A need to have her drive him mad like that till the end of time. He knew she would. Holding her half-mast gaze, he began pumping his hips, gliding forward and backward in a slow cadence at first until a tingling crawled up his back. Adjusting his pace, he gripped the nape of her neck, baring her down on him and pistoning deep inside her to a faster beat. The only sounds in the room were the hiss of their breaths, the grunts and moans of their desire, and the slap of skin against skin as they careened toward release.

Cassandra arched her hips to meet his every thrust, her inner muscles squeezing around him in a tight grip. Heat flooded his temples in a steady flow and his senses revved into overdrive. Perspiration glistened on their skin and the scent of her pleasure permeated the air around him. A groan rumbled deep in his chest. Trevor pressed a hand against her tight stomach and slipped the other between them. He strummed her clit in circular motions with the pad of his thumb. It didn't take long before she began contracting rhythmically around his cock and falling apart in his arms, throwing him over the edge into his own release.

"Fuck!" Trevor captured her mouth in a hard kiss and gripped her leg as he came, grunting with each pulse, each ripple of her body around his.

They held each other, mouths sealed, bodies undulating in the ancient dance until they both collapsed, spent, back against the smooth wooden surface. Trevor dropped his forehead to her breast and Cassandra cradled his head as their breaths sawed in and out of heaving chests. He eased back and held her warm whiskey-colored eyes with his. Their breaths mingled, their hearts beat in tune as he hovered his lips above hers, teasing her to nip at his. He thrust one last time and chuckled when her breath hitched. She shifted her hips and her inner muscles tightened around him in response.

"Ahh!" His eyes fluttered closed as a new surge of desire flickered inside him. "Tease."

"What? No seconds? Besides, look who's talking." Her snicker warmed him to the core.

Opening his eyes, he brushed the hair back from her forehead and laid a tender kiss on her swollen lips. He pushed up to rest on his hands and grinned down at her. "*A bhean*, a second helping of your mouthwatering treat would be deadly."

She snorted. "News Flash. Death by whipped cream. Empty whipped cream can found next to couple locked in deadly embrace." Trevor broke out in a fit of laughter and nuzzled her hand as she ran her fingertips down the side of his cheek. "It was lovely. I more than received my fair share." The smile in her sated, hooded eyes confirmed the veracity of her words.

"Glad to be of service." He helped her up and reached for his pants, zipping them as she scooted off the table in search of her own clothes strewn across the room.

"Go. Change into something comfy. I promised to take care of the mess."

"Damn, I knew there was a reason why I loved you."

Trevor covered his heart with his hand, feigning pain. "And I thought it was because of my sparkling personality."

"Keep thinking that, Boyo," she smirked over her shoulder as she headed up the stairs. At the top, she paused and glanced back down at him. "Hey, I need to go over the information Nate sent earlier. I should be done by the time you come up."

Trevor's grin faded as she disappeared from view. "Whatever it is, it better be damn important," he grumbled as he retrieved the fallen dishes, cleared the rest of the table, and loaded the dishwasher.

Chapter Four

Camel's Back

THE SHRILL RING CUT THROUGH Trevor's concentration. His eyes darted from the transcript on screen to the phone's call display. Cassandra's father. On the second ring, Trevor snatched up the wireless handset.

"Hi, Robert."

"Trevor. Is Cassandra around?"

"No, sir. She's out but shouldn't be long. Want me to tell her to call you as soon as she gets back?"

"No need. Just wanted to check in on her."

Trevor's brow creased. Robert still kept a close watch on their activities since the incident in France.

Knowing that Cassandra's father worried she would get hurt again under his watch hit a sore spot. Never again. He would do his damndest to keep her out of the line of fire—but his wife was feisty and had ideas of her own. Part of him doubted he could hold her back if a similar situation ever arose again.

Robert's comment only served to crumple his already ruffled feathers. "You don't need to keep tabs on her, Robert. I can handle that." His caustic tone reflected the toll his confidence had taken of late.

"I know but…she is my little girl."

Robert had made a big effort to bridge the gap between him and Cassandra since their move to Dublin. Distance made the heart grow fonder, and the saying seemed to hold true for Robert. Trevor would never do anything to derail those efforts, but Robert's lack of faith in him exacerbated his insecurities. He had struggled with doubts raised by the latest events—Cassandra's interest in ways to warm up their marriage, Nelson's sporadic yet unrelenting pestering. He lashed out in the worst possible way. "Glad to know you remember that," he said, prodding at Robert's own sore spot. Regret immediately wrapped its tight fist around Trevor's heart.

"Trevor—"

"Sorry. That was uncalled for."

"No, you're right." For a brief moment, a heavy silence filled the line as Robert searched for his next words. "When her mother died…a…a part of me died with her. Losing Cassandra would kill me. She's all I have left. I need to know she's safe, that she won't get hurt again."

Trevor drew in a deep breath. He understood Robert's pain. He had been dealing with his own for some time. "I get it. I won't let anything happen to her if I can help it."

"Exactly my point: can you?"

Robert's question sliced through him like a hot knife. Could he? Keep Cassandra safe? Would he be able to stop her from putting herself in danger for him again? Because of his need for closure?

"Your daughter is a very independent and strong-willed woman. I will never intentionally put her in danger. But I can't guarantee she'll accept sitting back at home if I'm sent out in the field or we're working a job."

"Talking about job…how dangerous can digital security be? I didn't think troubleshooting security systems involved daring situations. I mean, you and Cassandra should be able to handle everything from your desks, right? Technically, Cassandra should never encounter danger, which is a good thing. At least that's what Nathan says."

That name again. His mood soured considerably. "Been talking to Nelson, have you? May I ask what the topic of the conversation was?"

"The usual. He calls to ask after Cassandra. Talks about you."

In a flash, a flood of pounding heat travelled to Trevor's head. The direction of that conversation had taken a turn for the worst. "Really?" His tone was velvety smooth. "Why would Nelson discuss me with you?"

Trevor heard Robert inhale deeply. "Let's be honest here. For a while, they were close. I thought they'd end up together. It seems he hasn't yet given up hope that—"

"We both know that's not gonna happen," Trevor cut him off before Robert could finish his thought. His fingers drummed rapidly on the keyboard. A sick feeling flooded his stomach at the mere thought of what Cassandra's father had implied.

"I realized that the day we met. It was reinforced the day Cassandra took you for her husband." Robert's tone was appeasing.

Trevor pushed from his chair in frustration. A silence stretched between them as he paced the room with a heavy gait, trying to calm himself while searching for words.

After a few moments, Robert's voice broke the silence again. "Listen, Trevor. I don't want to create a chasm between us. I know you love her. I wouldn't be having this conversation with you if I thought differently."

"I love her more than life itself, so why the fuck are you questioning my ability to protect my wife?"

"I'm not. I keep an eye out for Cassandra the same way your parents would keep an eye on you if they were alive."

Trevor froze dead in his tracks. His heart sank low in his stomach and his ears rang with the echo of Robert's words. *If they were here, our lives would be completely different,* Trevor wanted to yell back, but he couldn't. That would open a new can of worms. Bring to surface things he wasn't prepared to share with Robert or anybody else at that moment. "I understand. Cassie is learning to accept that as a sign that you do care. Let me make this perfectly clear. My life's goal is to take good care of your daughter. Protect her at all cost. And, for the record, Nelson is an *eejit.*"

"I'm beginning to see that, son. What about your NSA job? Do you think there's a chance you might return to the States in the future?"

"No. The consulting position is just filler until our own business takes off. But maybe Cassie and I can carve some time out to visit soon. Bring you a taste of Ireland. Stephan has a bottle with your name on it."

Robert chuckled. "That would be nice. Looking forward to it. I'll let you get back to work. Tell Cassandra I said hello."

"Will do." Trevor stared at the handset, his mind processing the conversation. His grip tightened until his knuckles turned white. The rage he had held back boiled his blood and flashed through his entire body. He'd never experienced this kind of bone-crushing fury toward anyone in the past, but the last six months had taught him the true meaning of it.

His chest had churned with it the day Cassandra was injured and he had faced off with her attacker, Niklas Möeller. A similar rage seethed in his chest at that very moment. All because of Nelson's intrusion in their lives. The fucker had no right to meddle. No right to assume he could simply make a call and snoop. Yet he kept at it like a rabid dog with a bone. Trevor was reaching the limit of his patience with him. Soon enough, Nelson would add the last straw to his camel's back, and he worried about what the repercussions would be.

Trevor tossed the phone on the desk and dropped into his chair. *"Eejit,"* he muttered under his breath. His eyes flicked to the clock. Cassandra had been gone for a while and should be home anytime. Did she know Nelson was checking up on them? No. And, knowing Cassie, she wouldn't be too happy to find out about Nelson's indiscretions. But he also couldn't use that without sounding like a jealous crazed troglodyte.

He drew in a deep breath and released it slowly. The breathing exercise did nothing to take the edge off the frustration and anger wreaking havoc with his normally calm, carefree, happy-go-lucky self. *Shite!* He didn't want to face Cassandra in that shape. She would worry more than she did when he had one of his nightmares. He brushed his palms over his face and, without a second thought, headed for the gym in the basement. The punching bag—although a poor substitute for whom he'd rather beat to a pulp—should resolve his immediate problem.

Chapter Five

The Straw

TREVOR ROLLED TO HIS STOMACH and stuffed his head under the pillow in an effort to block the low buzz that had irritated him to awareness. Dawn blanketed the bedroom in semi-darkness. Way too early to face the day's duties. They had been out late with friends at the pub and had stumbled to bed wrapped in each other's arms only a couple of hours earlier.

Frustrated with the insistent racket, he yanked the pillow from over his head and rose to his elbows. "What the hell is that noise?" he asked out loud. "Cassie, what the hell is that?" He turned to her side of the bed and found her gone, the spray of the shower kicking on in the background indicating her whereabouts.

Pushing from the bed, he cocked his head and tracked the sound to

Cassandra's cell vibrating on the nightstand. *Who the hell?* He grabbed the phone and flipped it over. His eyes instantly narrowed to slits. His thumb hovered over the red ignore button but, on impulse, pressed the green instead. "You've got to be fucking kidding me."

Silence filled the space and then he heard an exasperated sigh. "Bauer. Is Cass there? I thought I called her cell."

"You did, Nelson." Trevor's voice still carried the hoarseness of the sudden awakening. "What's with the early call, mate? Do you know what time it is?"

"I do. I need to speak to Cass." Nathan's request sounded more like a demand to him.

"I thought you'd already done your monthly check." Trevor couldn't avoid the sarcastic tone from bleeding through.

"What do you mean?"

"Your call to Cassie a week or so ago, your regular calls to Robert." His casual mention was anything but. He intended it to be a warning that he was aware of Nelson's intrusion.

"Have you been listening in on my conversations? I could get you arrested for tampering with a CIA officer's phone line."

"Not my style. I trust the people around me to share that kind of thing with me. I know of your calls because there's nothing clandestine about it."

"Clandestine like the two of you skipping to France?"

Trevor breathed an exasperated sigh. "Here we go again. Like Cassie said, get over it, Nelson. She's made her choice. Leave it at that."

"No. She'll come to her senses. And when she does, I'll be waiting." Nelson's tone was smug, almost too confident. Trevor could have shrugged it off and put it down to Nelson's obsession, but Nelson had to open his mouth and continue with the jab. "We could've had something good going by now if you hadn't shown up in the picture when you did. *She was mine before you interfered.*"

Trevor's stomach churned. He had come to terms with the fact that Cassandra and Nelson had once been intimate before they had met. Prior to meeting her, he hadn't been a saint either. She regretted her choice and her guilt about that one night had tampered with her reason regarding Nelson's behavior toward her ever since. The idea that Nelson had laid hands on her, touched her, annoyed the crap out of him, but he could live with it. What cut him to pieces was the fact that Nelson expected, cheered, rejoiced even at the prospect that their marriage could fail. Trevor wondered how far he would go to get what he wanted.

Controlled anger pumped through Trevor's body. He ground his teeth as images of Nelson, a baseball bat, and him in an empty room crowded his mind. He held it in check. That wasn't him. He'd always handled conflict using sarcasm and wit as his weapons of choice. At least until Nelson had become a thorn in his side. He would not go down that dangerous road laden with rage and thoughtless acts. He needed to focus on finding the truth he sought, and on a more pressing matter—decoding his wife's sudden interest in new intimate fantasies.

But the hooligan in him couldn't let go of the need to come out on top, couldn't hold back the need for retaliation. Nelson had messed with his ego too many times in the past. He drew his guns and went on the attack.

His mellow brogue, edged with control, oozed sympathy. "Come to think of it, she did mention something about a poor experience she'd had just before she met me. I didn't realize that was you, mate. I'm sorry." A half smile quirked the corner of his mouth when Nelson's curse reverberated through the speaker. "Tell you what: Cassie has this nifty application to calculate the time difference between our zones. I'll email it to you. That way, the next time you feel compelled to call, you can be sure to do so at a more reasonable hour."

"Just put her on, Bauer." Trevor heard the steel running through his chilly tone. The CIA operative was good and ticked off.

"Not happening. She just stepped in the shower. Do you want me to give her a message when I join her? It must be extremely important for you to call this early."

"Just tell her I called," Nathan ground out so stiffly Trevor could swear he heard the grating of his teeth and the clanking of the rod up his ass across the line.

"Will do. She'll be tied up for a while though. I wouldn't wait by the phone if I were you." Trevor's smile slowly faded as Nelson hung up abruptly.

The bastard just didn't know when to quit. He had no regard for his and Cassandra's commitment. His refusal to acknowledge their marriage reminded Trevor of a child's belief that if one couldn't see it, it didn't exist. Trevor tossed the cell back on the table. The alluring sound of the running water beckoned him. He hadn't really intended to join Cassandra, but his body thrummed with nervous energy. There was no way he could go back to sleep. A mix of emotions prickled under his skin. The undeniable green luster of jealousy stood front and center. It aggravated his doubts, turning him into a powder keg ready to blow. With each step toward their bathroom, his need to take, plunder, and conquer grew exponentially.

Steam billowed above the shower enclosure and a glaze of foggy mist coated the glass door. The light above the stall outlined Cassandra's curvy silhouette through the haze. Trevor's arousal pulsed in response to the visual cue. His breathing quickened as his eyes traced the contours of her breast, hips, and long legs.

A rush of blood flowed through his veins straight to his groin, leaving him hard, ready, and all but drooling. Driven by a need to touch what that shadowy dream promised, he eased the shower door open and joined her.

She took his breath away. Facing the spray, eyes closed, hands buried in her hair, rinsing the lather from it, completely unaware of his presence in the large glass-walled shower. White foam trailed in little streams down her body, caressing her breasts and their dusky tips. He followed the trail of the bubbly water along the curve of her tummy, past her hips, over the dark curls blanketing her sex before running down her shapely legs to spill at her cute blood-red painted toenails. Trevor's lips ached to follow the same alluring path as the water.

His wife. His heart swelled with love at the same time thoughts of the little conversation they'd had a couple of days back and Nelson's call moments before swirled in his head like the steam billowing out the door into their room. His blood heated with male possessiveness and blinding fear. All he could think of was taking her, claiming her, marking her his so that no one could ever take away what they had found together, so that she would never forget what they had, so that she would not look at anyone other than him. For a brief moment, he questioned his motivation. *She was mine before you interfered.* Nelson's words popped in his head and erased any trace of hesitation. Unable to restrain himself one moment longer, he pounced on her, pinning her chest against the tiled wall with his body.

"Trevor!" Cassandra gasped, startled by his presence.

Trevor anchored his hands against the cold tile, caging her with his arms. He bit back a moan as his cock slipped between the slick warm cheeks of her ass. He nuzzled her ear while his hand of its own volition found its way to her round breast. A deep moan escaped his lips when her nipple beaded under his touch.

He kneaded her full breast, pinching her turgid nipple between his fingers, and Cassandra writhed under his touch, moaning in response. He lowered his head and murmured against her ear, "Good morning, *a ghrá.*"

Cassandra's breath caught at the contrast of the cool wall pressed against her front and his warm body against her back, the evidence of his arousal hot, firm, and probing against her ass cheeks. The reaction to his intrusion turned from surprise to a flare-up of desire in a matter of seconds.

She dropped her head back against his shoulder and, covering his hand with hers, pressed it harder on her breast. Shards of pleasure stabbed her. Her body quaked with each strum of his thumb across her sensitive nipple, with each flick of his tongue along the length of her neck. He nipped the tender flesh where it curved into her shoulder, sending liquid lava flowing through her already heated body to pool low in her belly, to pulse between her thighs.

With a shuddering sigh, she arched her lower body into him. She swallowed gulps of moist air and, reaching back, dug fingers deep into Trevor hips as she ground her ass against his groin. "Good morning to you, too. Did I wake you?" Her voice held a throaty quality.

Trevor groaned and shifted his hips to meet hers. Her question brought to mind the reason he was awake. The sway of her hips chased away the dark thoughts plaguing him. "Not really. I just woke missing you." He lowered his face and rasped in her ear. "You were already up, so I decided to hang out with my favorite person. Enjoy the heat and humidity in here."

Cassandra felt his warm breathy grin against her wet skin as he nuzzled her nape. Trevor's wicked humor, the one that always jerked her heartstrings, was hard to resist.

"What about you *a ghrá*? Are you hot and moist?" he asked, rubbing his cock down the crease of her ass to the wet folds of her sex, now slick with need.

She moaned low in her throat. His rubbing and teasing drove her to distraction. "It's definitely a little more humid in here since you decided to hijack my shower."

He chuckled and pressed firmer against her, forcing her flatter against the cool tile. She pushed back until their bodies melded skin to skin. Trevor turned on more nozzles and hot water cascaded over them from different directions, caressing her skin and slipping like warm tantalizing fingers down between her thighs.

Cassandra moved her hand from the tile to grip the back of Trevor's neck and turned her head, seeking his lips. "Trevor…" she breathed into the steam swirling around them. "Take me…now."

Her husky words fueled Trevor's compulsion to stake his claim to her. He craved to comply with her request in every single way imaginable and wanted nothing better than to thoroughly love this woman who'd turned his world upside down. His hand glided along her stomach and snaked further down to bury itself in the soft curls between her thighs, while the other palmed his hard shaft as he spread her legs with his knee and forced her to adjust her stance. He guided his throbbing shaft to her slick entrance, rubbing it against her folds while at the same time teasing her clit with the pad of his finger in slow, lazy circles.

"I want you inside me." Cassandra's gasped words hit him like a sucker punch to the gut. Blood rushed hot through his veins and into his cock. It jerked and pulsed in his hand. Positioning the engorged head against her slit, he buried himself deep inside her.

He hooked his arm under her knee, spreading her wider, and sunk into her warm depth again and again with long deep strokes, grinding his groin against her ass. The slap of their wet skin mingling with her mewls of pleasure only incited him to thrust faster, deeper. "Damn, woman… you feel so fucking good…you burn me alive," he hissed low in her ear.

A slow, drawn-out moan spilled from Cassandra's parted lips. A ball of heat rolled through her and settled on her clit, pulsing in tandem with the rocking of his hips. A twinge of need gripped her insides, tightening, squeezing his length, almost bringing her to her knees. She rolled her hips and raised her ass to meet his thrusts. "Trevor," she gasped. "I can feel every inch of you.

The rasp of cold tiles against her hard pointed nipples, the caress of the warm water trailing down their bodies, the touch of his fingertips to her swollen, throbbing clit all but seized her brain. "Faster!"

Trevor abandoned his titillating touch, wrapping his arm around her waist and hauling her tighter against him as their bodies collided in perfect synchrony. Her palm slid down the smooth tile and she replaced his touch with her own. She blew out a shallow breath as she slipped her fingers through her slippery folds and across her achy clit. Her hips bucked back against Trevor, who alternated his pace between deep and short, precise thrusts. Her heart raced and ragged breaths escaped her parted lips as her fingers rolled, rubbed, and pinched her over-sensitized nub. A tremor ripped a path of desire through her body. Craving more, she reached lower between her legs and brushed her fingers against his plundering shaft and along his sac.

"Fuck, Cassie! Yes, like that." His words were barely gasps. Electrical pulses travelled from his groin to his chest when Cassandra's feathery touch grazed his balls. She rolled them between her fingers, gently massaging, squeezing, and pulling at them. "God. That feels so good...." he rasped roughly, bucking against her.

"Trev." Her hoarse, broken voice, so full of need, slammed straight to his cock. Heart racing, he pulled from her, spun her around and into his arms. Eyes shut tight, he held onto her like a drowning man gripping a life vest.

"Trevor—"

"Shush." He kissed her lips. "Give me a sec. This is going too fast. I want it to last much longer." Trevor held her as he wrangled his desire. When he reined it under control again, he cupped her face and lifted it to his so he could look into her eyes. "Remember the other day when we discussed fantasies?"

Cassandra's eyes, glazed with desire, acknowledged his question. "Go on."

"I have one." He flashed a wicked grin. Interest flooded her eyes as her hands skimmed his back. He felt her heart jump in her chest and almost moaned when her lips parted in keen expectancy. He pulled back and searched her eyes. "Are you game?"

"I'm thinking—" She moved up to her toes and wrapped her arms around the column of his neck, "—I better start that blog this evening," she whispered and kissed him, plunging her tongue deep in his mouth.

He groaned and took control of the kiss, thrusting his tongue in deep exploration. Cassandra's hands slid to his waist and he walked into her until her shoulders pressed back against the tile. Gripping her round hips with both hands, he pulled her tighter against his groin and rubbed his hot flesh against her pelvis. Cassandra's whimper played to the rapid beat of his pulse, already racing out of control. He smoothed his palm along her tummy, down further still, searching and finding the soft bundle of nerves hidden there. He circled and rubbed his fingers along her clit, playing her like well-tuned guitar strings.

After months of careful discovery, he knew exactly how hard to press or how softly to graze to turn her wild, each guttural moan from her lips a confirmation he was on the right track. He slipped two fingers inside her, circling and pumping, coating them in her juices. Cassandra's breath broke in a sob and her mouth devoured his, sucking and licking, nipping and biting. His hips jerked and knees almost buckled when she sucked his tongue deep in her mouth. "I need to feel you around me again, Cassie!" he exhaled sharply, pulling from the kiss.

"Trevor." His name came out in a ragged gasp.

Leaning back, he tipped her face to his and stared into eyes gleaming with naughty invitation. *With you…anything.* Her words played in his mind once again; it was all the encouragement he needed.

His heart drummed in his ears as he, in a swift move, spun her around to face the smooth marble bench they'd installed in the shower during the renovations. "Bend over, *a ghrá,*" he urged, placing a hand and gentle pressure along her spine. Her gasp of surprise and little purr pushed his grin wider. "Hands on the bench, love."

He tugged her hips up, pressed between her shoulders for the right angle, and guided his cock back inside her, fully coating it in her slick juices before gliding it to the tight entrance of her ass. She gasped in surprise, her head snapped to him, eyes seeking his. His pulse stirred hot when he rubbed the glistening head of his cock against the puckered hole and pressed forward slowly while holding her fevered gaze. She gasped again, but didn't draw back. Trevor held his breath when he saw the unadulterated desire shining in her eyes. His heart almost burst when she reached back and grabbed his hip while pressing her ass gently against his throbbing cock.

"Don't hold back." She had no idea how sultry her voice sounded.

It was all the license he needed to proceed. The bottle of massage oil Cassandra kept in the shower would come in handy for what he had in mind. He squirted a liberal amount into his palm and spread it generously along his rigid aching length.

Savoring the moment, Trevor smoothed his hand down her back and ran his fingers down the crease from rosy rear hole to slit. His brow burned with the heat of anticipation. His breath huffed in and out of his chest as he circled the puckered skin of her ass and breached it with his finger, rubbing some of the oil onto the tight ring of muscles.

Cassandra's hips bucked against his hand. "Oh…," her breath escaped in a hiss.

He sucked in his breath, eased the finger further, and slowly pulled it out. Her head jerked back when he did the same with two fingers, wiggling them around, stretching the walls clamping down on them.

She cried out when he withdrew them and panted when he teased her, running his slippery length from her Venus dimples to her sex to thrust deep with quick hard pumps of his hips. Cassandra moaned, her breaths soft gasps of air as her inner muscles contracted around him. She groaned in protest when he pulled out again, dragging the head of his cock back between her cheeks.

Trevor pressed his palm between her shoulders again. "Lean down. Lift your ass for me," he rasped as he repositioned himself at the puckered flesh. "Relax, love. Let me in." Trevor found it hard to breathe as he pressed the pad of his thumb over the tight hole, rubbing and circling it, slipping its tip inside.

Cassandra moaned softly, gripped the marble bench with both hands, and, dropping her head forward, thrust her hips back. He positioned his hard shaft against the tempting entrance, gritting his teeth to keep himself from surging into her.

His legs trembled, his pulse raged, and control slipped as he forced his blood-engorged crown through her tight opening. He clamped down on the involuntary need to thrust and waited for her to relax the tight ring of muscles squeezing him like a vice. She was killing him softly.

She sucked in panting breaths and shifted her hips away from him. Trevor wrapped an arm around her waist. "Shush love, give it a second. Tell me what you need."

"Touch me." Arousal saturated her voice.

He didn't need any further direction. "Like this?" He slid his fingers across her clit, massaging it with a firm press of fingertips. Her body trembled and her muscles contracted around him. His breath seized in his lungs. A flood of pleasure coursed hot through him.

"Yes. Just like that."

When she relaxed her grip around him, he eased forward, strumming her swollen clit as he made the final push to the hilt. "That's it, *a ghrá*. God, you are so fucking tight." A hot river flowed in his veins, pounded in his head, his cock, and rippled under his skin. He was ready for the claiming. Ready for the branding. Ready to cross all lines to mark her as his.

His double assault left Cassandra trembling and weak at the knees. Heat pulsed through her with each brush of his fingers. Electric currents buzzed from her head to her toes. She clenched her muscles tight around him with need. She had never imagined the extent of the sensations blasting through her. His cock filled her, consumed her, and still she wanted more. Wanted to feel the novelty of that new friction, the bearing of his weight on her, the primal rhythm soothing the sensual burn. She wanted it all. She wanted to hear his grunts when he came inside her. "Trevor," she sobbed and arched her back, prompting him to begin rocking his hips.

Trevor expelled a rough breath, slid halfway out, and rammed back in, the mix of pain and pleasure so intense her vision edged with grey. Before long, his hips picked up speed, moving hard against her with each thrust while he continued his ministrations, replacing the initial discomfort with a molten need for release.

Cassandra's hand covered his and pressed his fingers harder against that sweet spot. Trevor played her engorged clit, rubbing, flicking across it with his elegant fingers just as expertly as they tapped his keyboard keys. "Yes, there. Right there. Faster. Harder." She wanted, needed to come. Trevor growled and increased his pace almost as if he could read her mind.

The hot water sluiced over them like another set of caressing hands, streaming from their bodies to the tiled floor. She matched each surge of his hips, each swipe of his fingers. Her clit throbbed beneath his touch. "Yes, yes!" The burn of a blinding climax ripped through her in pulsing ripples. "Cassandra, baby, I feel you."

Her lungs could no longer take in air and her heart jumped in an erratic beat in her chest.

"Close…so close," he hissed with each hard, deep thrust.

Cassandra almost missed his whispered words in the haze of her climax. Acting on instinct, she slipped her fingers inside her own sex and pumped in tandem to his thrusts. His cock brushed against them through her inner walls causing a tingling swirl to build in her belly. He seized her hips in a tight grip and continued his relentless assault, taking her to the edge again. "Come, love. I'm all yours."

Her voice, her words enveloped Trevor in a sensuous dream. Those few words that meant everything to him. The sensations were too much to bear. "Fuck, yes!" The harsh cry rumbled in his chest as he folded his body over hers. "Cassie, come again for me, lass," he breathed against her nape as he surged upward repeatedly. He knew she was close when the first ripples echoed and her muscles clamped hard around his cock.

"Trevor!" Her scream filled the steamy room as she rolled a second time over the edge. She threw her palms against the tile and pushed back with a sob. "I need to feel you come, too."

"Holy hell," he grunted, bucking out of control. The combination of the scent of her arousal, her wet skin against him, her eagerness to please, and her climax reverberating around him pushed Trevor further than he'd ever been before. A tingle flared at the base of his spine and his balls drew up. "Cassie!" He exploded inside her, coming hard and fast. Light-headedness overcame him as spurts of come jetted inside her hot tight channel and she contracted around his cock, milking him dry.

Trevor felt her sway and pulled her tight against his chest, twisting so he could collapse on the bench with her in his lap. Their bodies shuddered and melted against each other as their chests heaved, fighting for air.

"That...that was just...amazing." His voice, broken and ragged, expressed the full extent of the experience. After a few minutes, he gently lifted her off his groin, breaking their intimate connection, and cradled her in his arms. He lifted her chin and placed a kiss on her lips. "Let me soap you up, love. The water is cooling."

Cassandra moaned in protest. "Can't move anyway. All brain functions have stopped."

Trevor rose, set her gently on the bench, and paid her homage, chuckling as she complained when he lifted boneless limbs to soap and rinse her body reverently. Once finished to his satisfaction, he quickly washed himself and exited the stall, carrying her in his arms. He set her down to grab the closest towel and wrap her body in its huge fluffy softness before he carried her to bed. "Almost there, *a ghrá.*" His voice was low and husky even to his own ears.

Cassandra's body still shook with the fury of their lovemaking. She wrapped her arms around his neck and looked up to see a satisfied smile on his face. He caught her eye and pressed a kiss against her nose. Wrinkling it, she grinned weakly back at him. "Damn, Trevor. That was... intense. I don't think I can walk to the office just yet."

"Don't worry about that, *a ghrá.* We need to recharge," he insisted, pulling her close and cradling her within the band of his arms. The warmth of his body and the nest they cuddled in lulled her eyelids to drift closed. She snuggled closer, enjoying the caress of his hands on her hair, the soft touch of his fingers skating on her cheek, down her arms. "Yeah. Right. Recharge. Does that mean for more fun later or more work? Just asking...." Her voice trailed as her eyes drifted closed. "We'll need to talk about this sudden burst of creativity of yours."

He stilled and she opened them to meet his dark troubled ones. "What's wrong?"

"Nothing." His reply didn't match the expression on his face, nor the concern in his tone.

"We'll talk in a few hours. Once I can recover full use of my limbs. You used me well. No doubt about it." Leaning her head against his chest, she allowed the fast beat of his heart to lull her to sleep.

Chapter Six

Bring It On

TREVOR LAY IN BED STARING blindly at the ceiling. Even with Cassandra's warm body tucked at his side, even after the incredible experience they had just shared—because of it—his emotions were in turmoil.

He turned his head on the pillow and gazed at her. Her shallow, even breathing told him she had fallen back into a deep sleep. Slipping from the bed, he made a beeline to the kitchen. He grabbed a can of Guinness from the fridge and poured it into a pint glass. Regardless of the time of day, he needed it. Badly. His thoughts collided in his head as he waited for the foamy cap to form. What had he done? Had he finally screwed it up for good?

He set the pint on the coffee table and dropped to the couch with a deep exhale. The sun broke through the morning haze and brightened the ample sitting area as he stared into the void, thoughts lost in chaos.

He had given his inner fears free rein when he'd pushed Cassandra into giving in to his desires. Shame tightened a fist in his chest. He rested his head on the couch and squeezed his eyes shut. *What a fucking eejit I am.*

"What are you doing here? Is that beer?" Her voice cut through his wandering.

He jumped, almost knocking the glass over. "Fuck, Cassie. You scared the shit out of me."

"You didn't answer me." Uncertainty crowded her gaze when she pushed the glass aside and sat on the coffee table in front of him. Her voice carried a mix of irritation and hurt. "That's it. I've had it."

His heart sank in his chest like a brick. He closed his eyes, afraid to see the realization of his fears in hers, afraid to face the monster chasing his thoughts and which had apparently caught up with him.

"Don't," he pleaded softly.

"Don't?" Her eyebrows raised in inquiry.

"Don't give up on us." He stared into her eyes, hoping she could see the need, the helplessness mirrored in his. He couldn't think of living through another loss.

Her brow creased in a deep frown. "Give up? What the hell are you talking about?"

Surprise and relief slammed his senses into gear. "You're not leaving me?"

A droll look took over her features; at that moment he wanted to laugh at the beloved expression. "I thought...you were leaving me."

"Why would I do something so stupid as to leave the man I love, the one I risked everything for?"

"I thought I had taken my jealousy a little too far."

"Jealous? You?"

"I guess you could say insecurity, lack of self-confidence. Whatever you want to call it."

"Would you, the most confident, cocky person I've ever known, feel that way?"

"I might be confident about everything else, but when it comes to you...."

"You're joking, right?" Incredulity flooded her expression. "What the hell?" Comprehension filtered through when he didn't joke about it. She narrowed her eyes and shook her head. "You *are* serious."

"Don't look at me like that. See it from my perspective. Here's this woman. Beautiful, intelligent, strong-willed—everything a man could possibly dream of—and she takes notice of me. I've been told I'm not hard on the eyes, but come on, I'm no All-American. Yet she picks *me*. A desk jockey with enough baggage to load a whole seven-forty-seven. Shite, Cassie. I've put our lives on hold, for Christ's sake. And then there's the fact that I can't foresee if we'll succeed. Not knowing does a number with my head—and you worry about it. I know you do. To top it all off, we have no idea where my need for closure will lead us."

Cassandra's shoulders slumped and her hands wrapped around the edge of the table. "But what does that have to do with me leaving?"

He held her gaze. "Answer me this. Why are you so interested in finding ways to warm up our marriage?"

She rolled her eyes. "Wow. Answering a question with a question? Such a man."

"You're the one avoiding the question now."

She stared at him, emotions flipping through her eyes before she lowered them to her clasped hands. He hadn't missed her constant twist of her ring. "I..." she drew in a deep, ragged breath and darted her eyes back to his. "I worry that you'll get bored. That once you find what you're looking for, we'll drift apart. I'm trying to keep your interest alive."

His jaw gaped. He found himself speechless for the first time in forever. It dawned on him how ridiculous the situation was. He broke out in a fit of laughter. He laughed even harder at Cassandra's wide-eyed stare.

"What the fuck, Trevor. I just spilled my deepest fears and you laugh?"

He grabbed her and pulled her into his arms, still laughing, his face buried in her hair. Her fresh floral scent enveloped him and warmth radiated inside his chest. Once he could breathe again, he tilted her chin to him. "We are a good match, Cassie. We're both kinda fucked up in our own way, but we sure as hell fit together like yin and yang."

"You are still talking geek to me." She pulled back and Trevor could see the confusion still clouding his wife's eyes.

"*A ghrá,* since our wedding, I've wondered what I've dragged you into. I worry on a daily basis that I'm not the best thing that ever happened to you. The fact that I keep being reminded of that possibility is putting a serious damper on my self-esteem. Then you show up reading up on relationship advice—which didn't help, by the way. My first thought was that I was failing you somehow."

Cassandra's head reeled. She grappled with processing what Trevor had said. She thought of the many times she had struggled with self-esteem while working for her father. The need to make things right, to prove her worth, had put her on a collision course with Trevor. She remembered what it felt like to be challenged on things at which you excelled.

Trevor had been the one to make her see her own worth, to make her face who she was inside and value her strengths and weaknesses because they were all part of who she was. Realization slapped her upside the head. She let her gaze drift up to his and poured her love for him into his eyes, hoping he would get it once and for all. She placed her hand over his heart and tears burned in the back of her eyes. "You couldn't fail me if you tried."

He cupped her face and placed a soft kiss on her lips. His heart beat wildly under her palm. "I will never get bored with you," he retorted. "I want to grow old and wrinkly with you. I want to collect memories, good and bad, happy and sad, with you. I want to be the kind of father mine was, to our children. There is nothing else in this world I want more than a future with you—even closure; even finding the truth is not as important to me as you are. You carry my future in your hands, in your heart, Cassie girl."

He hated that he was the cause of the tear that slid from the corner of her eye. His pulse jumped when she placed his hand over her own heart. "And you carry mine in yours. Your needs are my needs. One day we'll find something that will break the case wide open. And we'll move on together when that happens—*whenever* it happens."

Trevor brushed his thumb across the wet track of the tear, wanting to erase it, and looked deep into her eyes. "You don't have to do anything special to keep me entertained." He kissed her soft, giving lips. His doubts had left him vulnerable to making mistakes. The biggest one of them was not trusting that Cassandra's feelings for him ran as deep as his for her. He'd missed a crucial detail, one he already knew. "I'm yours. You've branded me, mind, body, and soul."

"And you, me." He relaxed when Cassandra leaned into him.

"Just promise me one thing. We'll work on this connectivity issue we seem to have. My cryptography skills don't seem to quite work with your encoding. If I fuck up, just tell me straight up and I promise to do the same with you."

Cassandra grinned up at him, the teasing glimmer he adored shining from the depths of her warm brown eyes. "As long as you know deep in your heart and understand you are stuck with me forever, you have a deal, Mr. Brennan."

Adrenaline surged through his veins. "You know I love it when you call me that, don't you Mrs. Brennan?"

"Yes, I do, husband," she teased.

"Hmm…another of my favorite words. Say it again."

"Husband."

"Yeah, there it is." He took her hand and tugged her toward the stairs.

"Come. Back to bed. We need to recuperate from all this passion so early in the morning."

★ ★ ★ ★ ★

An annoying buzz woke him again hours later. He checked the time on his cell phone. Noon. Shite. They'd slept in. George would be at his office by then, probably antsy to discuss the case they had going and the possible trail Trevor had found the day before. His brows knit together as the noise continued, this time coming from Cassandra's nightstand. Her phone. The replay of the morning's events ran through his head as he reached over her sleepy figure to grab her cell.

He stared at the number on the display and the absence of anger he felt brought a smile to his face. Slipping off his side of the bed, he pressed the green button. "Nelson. Great to know you got the time-zone thing down." Nelson would always rub him the wrong way, but Cassandra had reinforced Trevor's foundation, helped him build tall walls, and renewed his confidence.

"Bauer. Are you Cass' answering service now?"

"Funny guy. Hold on." Trevor muted the phone, rounded the bed, and woke Cassandra with a kiss. "Wake up, sleepyhead. Your buddy Nelson is on the phone."

"You've got to be kidding me," she grumbled, covering her face with the pillow. "Take a message."

Trevor laughed and shook his head. "Nope. You better take it before he thinks I've got you hogtied in the basement."

"Hmm…good that sounds. That thought you should hold."

Her muffled Yoda impression brought a smile to his face and, with a chuckle, he handed her the phone and headed to the door. "Bring it on."

THE END

NOTE FROM THE AUTHORS

We sincerely hope you enjoyed these Countermeasure Bytes of Life. We'd appreciate if you:

LEND IT – to friends and family.

REVIEW IT – at the site you purchased it from. Positive reader reviews have a huge impact on the success of a book.

RECOMMEND IT – to all of those you think would enjoy it. Positive recommendations from friends are the number one decision maker for many readers, in regard to trying authors unknown to them.

Craving more?
Don't miss the next novel in the
hot and thrilling
Countermeasure series

A preview of

TO RUSSIA WITH LOVE

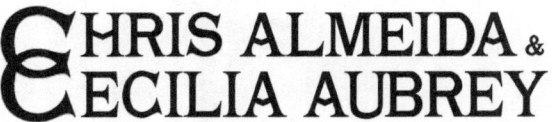

Prologue

Chicken-scratch

"SO, HOW IS THE NEW guy doing?" Roy Denner, Chief Financial Officer of Mark Devlin Software, asked Mark Devlin, owner of MDS. They often held their casual meetings over the phone, and that day was no different.

"New guy? Oh…you mean Antonín Mucha? Amazing. He had an impressive resume. Worked with some big names, including Conor Brennan." Over the line, Roy heard Mark take a sip of his coffee.

"Brennan? Why is the name familiar?"

"Big name in biometrics. He led some major projects in the field."

"Ah."

"Mucha helped him with an algorithm for voice recognition some years back."

"I see."

"Apparently they were close for a while. Mucha mentioned he had some of Brennan's notes. I bought them from him. They will be worth a fortune down the road—even though they look like chicken-scratch to me."

"Why?"

"Don't you remember? Brennan died in a boating accident some five years back—"

A knock on Mark's door sounded over the line.

"Hi, Paul. Everything okay?" Roy overheard Mark's question followed by a pause, then Paul's muffled reply in the background.

"The decrypter, Mr. Devlin…I don't know how…the files are gone." Paul Faber, the lead developer at MDS, was in charge of their main piece of software—which was also one of his projects from inception.

"Mark, what's going on?" Roy asked over the line.

"Roy. Grab Harold and get over here. My office. We have a situation." His voice was thick with tension.

Mark hung up and Roy immediately called Harold Preston, MDS's head of security, and instructed him to meet them at Mark's office on the double. It was going to be a hell of a day.

★ ★ ★ ★ ★

George scanned the latest assignments and prioritized their order of attack for the day. It would be handled as soon as he could get a hold of Trevor.

With that in check, he scanned the latest report generated on their little keyword list—something he had been keeping an eye on for his buddy. He had to take a second pass at it to make sure he had gotten it right. When he did, a small smile played on his features.

"Trev's going to want to hear this one…"

More books in the
Countermeasure series
and
Countermeasure: Bytes of Life series:

UNCHARTED
COUNTERMEASURE
ECSTASY BY THE SEA
CUFFED AT MIDNIGHT
PASSION AT DAWN
TO RUSSIA WITH LOVE
BLINDSIDED
LOST TO RAPTURE
ALTERNATE CONNECTION
BOUND BY LOVE
LONDON BY MOONLIGHT

ABOUT THE AUTHORS

CHRIS ALMEIDA & CECILIA AUBREY

Writing had touched Chris Almeida's and Cecilia Aubrey's lives in different ways through the years but had never taken flight until 2010, when Chris and Cecilia met and began role-playing online as a hobby. It was through playing fictional characters in a sort of improv written theater, that writing took a central position in their lives. The transition from role playing to novel writing was smooth and they attribute the ease of writing realistic characters to their ability to live the scenes 'through role play.

Chris and Cecilia have since chosen to release all their titles independently. They have several short stories and two novels published under their own label, Éire Publishing, and are vocal supporters of independent publishing done right. They are currently working on the next novel in their series. Through all the chaos and laughter, they still hold true to their roots, bringing their favorite role-play characters and stories to life.

Be sure to connect with them online!

To remain updated about new releases, subscribe to their newsletter:

http://chrisalmeida-ceciliaaubrey.com/about/newsletter

You can find updated information about the authors and the upcoming books at:

http://chrisalmeida-ceciliaaubrey.com

http://countermeasureseries.com/

http://www.facebook.com/Counter.Measure.Series

http://www.facebook.com/CAlmeida.CAubrey.Authors

http://twitter.com/CAlmeidaCAubrey